Born a few years after the Second World War into a society that is unrecognisable today, Ed Johnson has seen and lived through the changes, which he, in part, gives as one of the reasons he decided to start writing.

His working career has been in electronics and technology; mending a computer in 1970 was a very different experience from working with them today.

He says he is lucky with his life experiences. In the 1950s, you were expected to be able to turn your hand to anything, which, again, he says, has contributed to his writing.

Ed Johnson

Why Am I Here?

Jane's Story

AUSTIN MACAULEY PUBLISHERS
LONDON • CAMBRIDGE • NEW YORK • SHARJAH

Copyright © Ed Johnson 2024

The right of Ed Johnson to be identified as author of this work has been asserted by the author in accordance with sections 77 and 78 of the Copyright, Designs and Patents Act 1988.

All rights reserved. No part of this publication may be reproduced, stored in a retrieval system, or transmitted in any form or by any means, electronic, mechanical, photocopying, recording, or otherwise, without the prior permission of the publishers.

Any person who commits any unauthorised act in relation to this publication may be liable to criminal prosecution and civil claims for damages.

This is a work of fiction. Names, characters, businesses, places, events, locales, and incidents are either the products of the author's imagination or used in a fictitious manner. Any resemblance to actual persons, living or dead, or actual events is purely coincidental.

A CIP catalogue record for this title is available from the British Library.

ISBN 9781035810000 (Paperback)
ISBN 9781035810017 (ePub e-book)

www.austinmacauley.co.uk

First Published 2024
Austin Macauley Publishers Ltd®
1 Canada Square
Canary Wharf
London
E14 5AA

Thanks to my wife who has pestered, cajoled and helped me to get this book published.

Table of Contents

Jane's Story	13
Tony's Story	30
Naomi's Story	40
Private Detective Steve Morris' Story	43
Naomi's Story	44
Mark (the Vape) Story	47
Carl's Story	50
Mark the Vape	52
The Television News	54
Mark the Vape	55
Tony's Story	56
Jane's Story	60
Tony's Story	63
Carl's Story	64
Naomi's Story	66
The Television News	69

Carl's Story	70
Naomi's Story	71
Carl's Story	72
The Television News	74
Mark the Vape and Uncle Bob	75
The Television News	76
Carl's Story	77
Mark the Vape and Uncle Bob	78
Tony's Story	79
Uncle Bob and 'the Boss'	81
Tony's Story	82
Carl's Story	83
Naomi's Story	85
The Television News	86
Naomi's Story	87
Uncle Bob and One of His 'Sub Contractors'	89
Detective Inspector Will Knowles and Detective Sergeant Fred Wills Midlands Police	91
Carl's Story	94
Detective Inspector Will Knowles and Detective Sergeant Fred Wills	97
Uncle Bob and Mark the Vape	98

Detective Inspector Will Knowles and Detective Sergeant Fred Wills	99
Jane's Story	101
Uncle Bob and Mark the Vape	104
Jane's Story—With Detective Inspector Donald Jones in London	105
Carl's Story	107
Detective Inspector Will Knowles and Detective Sergeant Fred Wills	108
Carl and Detective Inspector Will Knowles	110
Uncle Bob and His IT Sub Contractor	111
Carl and Detective Inspector Will Knowles	112
Carl and His Solicitor	113
Detective Inspector Will Knowles and Detective Sergeant Fred Wills	114
Uncle Bob and His IT Sub Contractor	115
Uncle Bob and Mark the Vape	116
Naomi's Story	117
Private Eye Steve Morris	118
Detective Inspector Will Knowles and Detective Sergeant Fred Wills	119
Carl's Story	120
Carl and Naomi	121
Naomi and Detective Inspector Will Knowles	122
Detective Inspector Will Knowles and Detective Sergeant Fred Wills	123
Carl's Story	124

Carl and Naomi	125
Naomi's Story	126
Carl's Story	127
Jane's Story	129
Naomi's Story	131
Jane, a Constable and Detective Inspector Will Knowles	132
Detective Inspector Will Knowles and Detective Sergeant Fred Wills	133
The Police—A Little Later	135
Jane's Story	137
Uncle Bob and Mark the Vape	138
Uncle George and the Boss	139
Naomi's Story	141
Carl's Story	142
Jane's Story	145
Jane and Mike	146
Naomi's Story	148
Detective Inspector Will Knowles	149
Naomi's Story	151
Private Detective Steve Morris	152
Private Investigator Steve Morris with Mark the Vape	153
Mark the Vape and Uncle Bob	154

Steve Morris	156
Mary Following Naomi	157
Mark and Mary	158
Mary	159
Mary and Private Investigator Steve	160
Description of Following Naomi	161
Mary's Story	162
Private Investigator Steve Morris	164
At the Police Station—DI Will Knowles and DS Fred Wills	165
Detective Inspector Will Knowles and Detective Sergeant Fred Wills	166
Phone Call to Jane from the Police	167
At Jane's Flat	168
Jane's Story	170
Detective Inspector Donald Jones	172
Jane's Story	173
Private Detective Steve Morris	174
Police in Kent	176
Police Station in Kent	178
Police Station in Kent	180
Uncle George and the Boss	181
Naomi's Story	184

Jane's Story	186
Detective Sergeant Fred Wills and Detective Constable Susan Howe	187
Jane's Story	188
DI Donald Jones and Detective Constable Susan Howes	189
Naomi's Story	190
Carl's Story	191
Naomi's Story	195
Detective Inspector Will Knowles and Detective Sergeant Fred Wills	196
Mark the Vape and Uncle Bob	198
Naomi's Story	200
Jane's Story	201
Detective Inspector Will Knowles and Detective Constable Susan Howe	204
The Police Meeting	206
Carl's Story	207
Carl's Story	209
Jane's Story	210
Carl's Story	211

Jane's Story

I still ache. My shoulders feel like they have been beaten, my neck is in knots and it hurts to turn it. I am cold. I have been here three days now. I wish I was warm and comfortable like I was before this nightmare started. Each day, I wake and feel the same. I remember each day that I am in jail. I ask 'why am I here'. I feel groggy, almost hung over.

I now realise again that this is serious; I could spend the rest of my life in a foreign jail.

Why am I here?

Tony. Tony has disappeared. He went off to work while I went on the jeep safari. But he didn't come back and the maid reported the blood, and then the police arrived.

Why? I didn't do anything, but how do I prove that. What went wrong? I must try and work out what happened. It has only been five days since we met; I will go over it and try and work out what has happened before they come and get me for 'questioning'.

So five days ago, I was at Gatwick waiting for Easyjets premium travel experience to Faro. I nearly had to give it up as my phone went missing, luckily someone at the gym handed it in. I don't remember putting it down but I was doing a very extreme workout that day.

All was going well. The train was on time, check in took no time at all and I got a glass of quite palatable Pinot Grigio waiting for a call that never came, but by careful attention, I saw that the gate was open.

The stroll down was improved by seeing that the snivelling child who had been getting attention from most of the departure area was on another flight. Adding pleasure was the three lads who had been giving my legs far too much attention. One had knocked over his and a mate's beer while staring in my direction in the bar.

They were on the flight with the screaming child. Their slightly inebriated state mixed with the child and a mother who refused to say anything more than 'quiet now; what's the matter' classic.

But not on my flight! So my boarding card checks out OK at the gate and I sit for what I am told will be ten minutes. Now how much better can life get? The good looking, fit looking, very clean looking guy? OK I fancied him on sight. He was just my type; broad smile, broad shoulders, expensively dressed, the check in girl almost wet herself when he started joking with her.

It always amazes me how stupid women are when they come into contact with a great looking guy. I, however, know by default that the chances of anything happening are very small. *That is the first thing that is wrong.* Why did he sit next to me?

There were several better looking women who gave him the once over, I did as well, but I did it surreptitiously, not blatantly like the blonde with the plastic tits who gave him a look that said the mile high club was on if he wanted it.

"Excuse me, can I sit here?" Foreign tinge to the accent and the cologne was not overpowering.

Indeed it must have been so expensive that it made me say, "Of course, how could I stop you?" I know I should have not looked directly into his eyes and I should not have used that flirty tone.

"I bet you could pick me up and chuck me through the window," he laughed. The way he ran his eyes over me didn't do my ego any harm either as he said it. I know I am pretty fit but I didn't think it showed. *Actually, it does not show so how did he know?*

Now I am not a slapper; yes, I do like men. Well, I like them a lot and I am not averse to the occasional 'liaison' as they say. I have had about three boyfriends this year (OK five) but that is only one a month. All right, the first four were in January but I have been going steady since early February. Why am I going away on my own you might ask and flirting with a stranger.

That would mean going back too far; for the moment I need to remember something to give the police. I am sure that having a fling with a married man didn't make another man disappear. We only meet two lunchtimes a week. An ideal situation as I work freelance and can do all the work I miss in the evenings and I get to go out and party without any of that pressure of a proper boyfriend. Can't dance with anyone else, can't have a fun snog, well you know.

So at the airport, he introduces himself, asks if I am travelling with anyone, but very politely. Asks if it's OK to try and sit together, "I will completely understand if you don't want to." Good heavens, is this man too good to be true. He chooses me over plastic tits and still wants to be the perfect gentleman.

I demurely agree we can sit together. Now it's my turn to act a bit more properly. I don't jump on men that fast, but I am certainly not letting this one get away if I can help it.

We board, the usual scrum for the best seats; he leads me towards the least populated area and we get two together.

"How do you do, my name is Tony."

"How do you do, my name is Jane."

"Well, I know you are going to Faro," he laughs, I don't, it brings him up short. "Sorry, I do sometimes make stupid jokes like that. I am on a last minute trip, some business but hopefully not too much. I am staying in Portimao but my business is in Faro. I don't like to be too close to where the business is. It can make it too easy for decisions to be changed if the client can meet you in the street."

That's better, strangely I am staying in Portimao as well I got a good deal out of lastminute.com. "I am staying at the Rivero." I know there are lots of hotels so there is little chance that he will say;

"That is quite a coincidence I am staying there as well." He says it with surprise and I see some delight in his eyes. This is looking quite sweet.

"What do you do?" He is changing the subject but again, I sense that this is because he does not want to be too forward. Wow, a good looking stranger for the weekend. My mind drifts off into three lazy days of more pleasure that I could have anticipated. I see…Actually, what I see is him looking quizzically at me as I have been dreaming for about thirty seconds and must look pretty stupid.

"I am a fashion and homeware engineer." He looks at me very puzzled. "Well you asked and I was trying to come up with a simple way of explaining."

"What I do is take a new product, analyse it and get it made with either fewer or simpler parts so it costs less to manufacture. I have to do this in hours so that the design can be sent to India or somewhere similar, and made, shipped back to the UK and sold. My input is usually an intense and very short period. If the product looks like it will be one that continues, then I do get longer to do the redesign."

"That sound fascinating, but why you?" Here the look says the same but he qualifies quickly. "What I mean is, are you an engineer or a fashion designer? It is a strange mix. Am I wrong or missing something?"

"No, not at all. I did a mechanical design engineering degree at university and made stupid clothes as a side line. The clothes became easier as I understood basic manufacturing principles of simplicity and ease of manufacture."

"Sorry, you have lost me. I can't understand why a designer can't design a dress properly."

"Maybe not too many dresses, but I do a lot of the engineering for high heel shoes. I come up with simpler ways of getting the strength they need but cheaper to make. The last ones used coloured carbon fibre, the whole shoe was made of it and as the top was a weave it meant that we had them made in an autoclave the same as a formula one racing car."

Now he started to look impressed, and as we were on my favourite subject, me, I carried on.

"Another one that went well was a range of sports shoes that used asymmetric colouring, by making a part that had one colour on the inside and another on the outside and could be turned inside out. We only had to make one part not two. Over a million trainers that can save 50p each and I get 5%."

Now he looked really impressed and I almost let him start talking but I was now in motor mouth mode.

"So I had to patent that idea before someone stole it and I now get a small cut on every trainer it is used on."

I know it was boasting but I did get about ten grand a year for that idea. A small warm feeling came over me and I paused enough for him to open his mouth.

"Drinks, sandwiches, tea or coffee?" Perhaps the best Essex accent I had heard for a long time.

"Would you like a drink?" He was asking me.

"G & T please," I said fumbling for my handbag. By the time he had said 'two', he had managed to palm a note to the lovely orange lady (Easyjet remember) and given her a nod that said keep the change before I got the clasp open.

"That was kind. But I want to pay you back. I don't know you and I don't like taking drinks from strangers."

"By all means, you can meet me for a drink in the bar."

"That was a smooth move. Now you have me meeting you tonight, how do you know I don't have a date?" A cloud passed across his face, he looked sad! I took pity. "I don't have a date so yes I will buy you a drink." A broad smile now and what seemed unusual a look of elation.

That was wrong as well it was not a look of elation, only relief, I realise that now.

I had him on the back foot so I went in for the kill. "What do you do then? Where are you from? Why have you not got a date?" I know the last one was unnecessary but I could not resist, I was beginning to have a good time.

He reeled back in mock fear. "Too many questions! Name rank and serial number only! OK in reverse order." He paused and took in a deep breath. "You are really too much you know, questioning me like that!"

"I don't have a date because I was planning a quiet weekend relaxing, one meeting only. I have been working too hard recently. I am from Latvia. I deal in luxury cars, moving them from where they are cheap to where they are expensive."

He stuck his tongue out at me and gave me a weird, cross eyed look. I laughed.

"Touché," I laughed again. "That was very good and again very smooth. I shall have to watch you!"

Now he was laughing and I felt that I did really like him. Not perfect you understand, but good looking in a designer stubble sort of way and with the ability to take the mickey out of himself. Being foreign and little mysterious, meant he was intriguing, almost a hint of danger. Inside, I shivered with anticipation.

"So do you have transport to the hotel?"

"I have a car booked if you want to share, unless you want to pay the extra for a taxi or get the bus?" Suddenly, he was being practical, not sure I liked this but I was not turning down a free ride, it must have shown though.

"Sorry," he said. "I should have said that later or better. It came out badly as if I am trying to kidnap you."

"NO, that is fine. I don't get a free taxi as part of my package. Did you do a last-minute thing as well?"

"No, I arranged this weeks ago, it's not easy to get." A pause as he seemed to be struggling for words. "Everything how I like it when you book late." *That was a bit cagey,* I thought. Am I missing something?

"Ladies and gentlemen, the captain has switched on the fasten seatbelt sign. Can you return to your seat, fasten your seatbelt and put your tray in the upright position."

"Wow, that went fast," we both said together and laughed. "The two hours have flown past. No pun intended," he said, more laughter and a dirty look from plastic tits as well!

The plane banked and we were treated to the usual view of the sea then we were bumping along. *"Welcome to Faro. The time here is 14:35. The same as the UK and the outside temperature is 24 degrees."*

That's better than the ten in sunny Gatwick I said, he pushed himself back in his seat and smiled.

We disembarked, got on the bus and swayed to the terminal trying not to fall over as the bus hared around the tarmac. I felt a firm hand on my shoulder that steadied me and I managed to blush!

The sign said 'Carros de luxo' and the young guy who met us was well dressed, no jeans, a nice suit; another Mr 'perfect designer stubble'. The 'car' was a quite something as well; a large Merc with a personalised plate and a proper uniformed driver as well as the guy who had met us in the hall. I raised my eyebrows at him.

"I deal in exotic cars. The guys I work with make sure I am looked after."

We were whisked away and I asked, "So how do you make money moving cars?"

"Like your simple, but clever, ideas this one is easy. The tax regimes in different countries change the value of a car. So here in Portugal, it is very expensive to bring in a top end BMW or one like this. But if its three years old, then the rules are different. So we wait until a dealer has not met his targets for a month and pick up a new car for less than it cost him."

"We say we are exporting it and get the tax and duty back and its kept in a secure pound. Then when it is just under three years old, we export it. The client will have paid for it when we buy it. Sometimes, they even come to the store and have a little drive! We have buyers in all the major European countries and get the cars that are the specification the customer wants."

"All legal and any recession actually boosts our sales as people with money don't like 'second-hand' cars and also hate paying tax. The slump just increases our margins as the dealers dump the cars."

I looked impressed as I guess that with a luxury car like the one we were in costing maybe £100K, it must be a big money business. But I thought to myself, *For once shut up and keep quiet.* There may be secrets that I should not hear.

The Rivero website looked good on the net but the back of the hotel looked dire. Yes, you could see the sea, or was it an estuary, as we drove close, but it was not impressive, neither was the room I had overlooking the pool. That was the view, OK but I guess that is last-minute thing.

We parted in reception; he being welcomed like royalty, me being left with a trolley thing for my bag. Ho hum. We were to meet at eight in the bar and he had said perhaps we could have dinner. Again he slipped into the slightly, what I now was considering shy, manner he had. I said that would be fine.

Well, a swim and walk around revealed a small area of shops and restaurants, some with sea views, some overlooking a marina. Then, the torturous job of getting ready for the evening. With only a small case of clothes that would probably only just be good enough. Still the killer heels usually work and I keep the legs toned and that is usually enough to create an illusion.

At five past eight, he was not in the bar, so I ordered a G & T and he walked up behind me saying, "Sorry, sorry I just went to your room to escort you and must have just missed you." True or not, back to very smooth. He accepted the drink and I put it on my room bill.

We went to sit in a comfortable area overlooking what I now knew was the estuary, this was better. I asked, "Does the restaurant have a view as good as this?"

"Where I plan to eat is better." I looked at him puzzled as I could see the restaurant behind him and was really asking if he had got us a good table.

The menus arrived and I was beginning to feel disappointed. We chose and he ordered a bottle of very good wine.

We made small talk as we waited for the 'call' to our table. It didn't come as you would normally expect. The barman came over and said he had just been told our first course would be ready in ten minutes and would we care to get seated.

Completely bamboozled now, I was led away, up some stairs and through a door that looked like a room door but with a logo rather than a number. Into a living room with a table set up for dinner. I realised that I was in his suite.

"That is very sneaky." I wandered around as he opened the wine and poured two glasses. We looked at the view and watched a yacht struggling against the tide.

There was a knock at the door and it opened and a waiter brought in the starters, put them down and discreetly left.

"I don't know what to think. You pick up a poor girl at the airport, now this!" I flung my arm around.

"Tell me it's better than a dinner alone please?"

"It is beautiful, thank you; how could I fault it? That is the problem. Girls like me don't get this lucky." Did I really say that. It must have been the gin, the wine or maybe I really meant it.

"Girls like you, beautiful, fit and confident are what I like. I can't stand tacky and I am actually not too comfortable here. There are too many women, or rather their men, who have bought their bodies from a plastic surgeon. Too many men who make a life out of playing golf, so I do lock myself away a bit. You are a breath of fresh air, so thank you for accepting me."

Ya boo sucks, I thought to plastic tits and I smiled, a big happy smile. It was going to be a great evening.

"Cheers." Glasses chinked and we sat. The food was very good. I somehow wondered if it was better than what we would have got downstairs. I didn't mind at all! The starter was cleared, the main course and dessert were superb, the talk very light and we went through music (pop to classical), film (something with a story that engages), food (most cuisines), sport and fitness were where we were closest. He was gym, running and badminton, where I am gym, running and cycling. I teased him that he probably got driven all the places that I cycled to.

We seemed to be very similar about likes and dislikes on a lot of things; not perfect but probably as perfect as any man I had ever tried matching myself to. I was very relaxed and waiting for him to make a move, which when he did, I was again surprised.

There was a distant noise of party music. Tony said, "How about a dance then?"

"Where?"

"Here, downstairs by the pool. They have a small band and that big patio area will be a dance floor by now."

We danced for an hour, drank a non-alcoholic cocktail which surprised me. I even asked him why he was not trying to get me drunk.

Before he could answer, the music went slower and he offered me his arms. *Careful now*, I thought, but still went right in close.

"I don't want you drunk, I want you…" A pause. "Well, I just want you." Bang just like that.

"There was Mr smooth again. I will let you know soon." I hugged closer and shivered.

"Are you cold, do you want to go indoors?" We were back to Mr concerned and practical. It almost broke the romantic moment, but it did prompt my decision and I grabbed the back of his neck and kissed him. He almost recoiled in surprise, I sensed, then relaxed and enjoyed it. So did I.

He stared into my eyes and I thought I almost saw a tear. "Tonight?"

"Maybe," and we kissed again.

He took me by the hand and led me indoors. I expected him to try and take me upstairs, but we ended up in an unpopulated part of the bar.

"Believe this or not, I am nervous. I don't usually try and get girls into bed on a first date, so I am sorry I asked you. I just couldn't resist. Sorry."

I looked him in the eye carefully, waited a good ten seconds and pinched him very hard on the inside of his thigh. He screamed and then cut himself off so as not to attract attention. I laughed and rubbed where I had pinched and slid my hand higher.

"We only have three days and if you think I am going to waste any of it, you have got to be joking."

He took my hand. "One more dance then." I was reluctant and rather taken aback, even a bit annoyed. He was being a bit bossy, I thought. He probably thought he was being romantic.

On the dance floor by the pool, he took me in his arms and I put mine around him. We danced and I got my hands down by his lovely tight bum. He moved closer and I picked him up got him on my shoulder and dumped him in the pool before he knew what was happening.

The people around us and the staff did what I think would be called a sharp intake of breath. Tony surfaced and tried to offer me his hand to get out, I stood there.

"I am not coming in there with you." I laughed and beckoned him to follow me. I was in front by six feet, out of reach. I ran up the stairs with him gaining. I got to the door in time to use the key card I had quietly removed from his jacket pocket in the last dance. For once, the door opened straight away and I was in before he got to me. I ran straight to the bedroom and got out of my dress before he caught me.

"I can't get that dress wet, it's the only one I have here." I laughed as we embraced and I felt the water from his hair dribbling down my back as he leant me back against the bed, putting his hands all over me stroking very firmly and with a passion I was looking forward to returning.

Nothing more was said. He undressed, hung his wet clothes on a door and grabbed me. An hour later, we kissed a last time and fell back. I was asleep in seconds, my fingertips just touching his.

BANG! The cell door opened. "I trust you slept well?"

"No, hardly at all."

"Well, enough to answer some questions I hope. Your lawyer is here to see you before the formal interview."

I was led to an interview room with recording equipment and sat there was the greasiest looking guy I had probably ever seen. His suit needed cleaning, the jacket collar looked caked and when he offered me his hand, I nearly recoiled, but this guy was on my side it seemed. He had a slight stammer which hid some of his accent.

"My name is Jose and I am your appointed lawyer. Do you have any objection to me representing you? If you have your own lawyer then that is fine as far as I am concerned. If not, I had better warn you that you are in serious trouble. Are you aware of that?"

I nodded and replied that I was happy with him, but I could not understand what evidence there was against me. Did he know?

"Yes, I have seen the preliminary report, it seems very concise and complete; you look very guilty. Tell me your side and I will see if I can find any chinks in their armour. It won't take much to get this down to manslaughter."

"But I am not guilty. I didn't do it!"

"Perhaps not, but my job is to get the best result for you. Of course I will try and get you off, but if I were you, I would be prepared for ten years. Well, that is twenty and it will get reduced for good behaviour. Tell me what happened from your side and I will tell you what the police are surmising, but be quick we have an hour before your interview."

So I sketched over the last three days, the meeting, the dinner and the dancing.

The morning was the usual slightly embarrassing 'hello' but there was no ice to break and over a light breakfast, served in his suite again. We did a bit more 'investigating' of each other and Tony asked if I knew the area.

"No, I have never been to Portugal before. Do you?"

"Well, I have been here, but never taken the time to investigate. Do you fancy hiring a car and doing some sightseeing?"

"Yes, that would be brilliant. Where shall we go?"

"No idea. I will phone and book a car and ask the people at reception."

"I have a problem, my clothes are all in my room and I am going to feel so embarrassed hobbling round in high heels and a short dress."

Tony took my hand and led me into the suite's other bedroom. My case was beside the bed, my clothes were hanging in the wardrobe and my cosmetics were on the dressing table.

"Back to Mr smooth I see." I smiled. Tony was by that point asking for a car and what was worth seeing.

I was feeling elated and a little confused. Things were happening fast but in a way that I liked. It was almost too good to be true how well it was going. *That was part of what was wrong; it was too good to be true!*

So dressed in shorts and a t-shirt in ten minutes, I was ready. The car hire people sent a car straight over and off we went. "Where are we going?"

"To the brewery." I could not see his eyes as he said it because of the wrap-around sunglasses but I could guess he was smiling at my dilemma. How do you ask what brewery without seeming to like breweries, like the old question 'which of these sheep are most attractive'; the answer being none of them.

"OK where is this brewery exactly?"

"Sagres." (Sounded like Sagresh)

"Why are we going to a brewery?"

"We are not exactly going to a brewery." He handed me a map and when I had unfolded it for the fourth time, it showed me where we were and I found Sagres.

"OK I can see where this place is, so why are we going?"

"Have you been to Lands End in Cornwall?"

"No."

"Well, soon you will be at lands end in Portugal. I wanted to be beside the sea but not just a boring beach."

Now, I was handed a guide book and while my gorgeous driver threaded his way around the outskirts of Portimao, I read about Sagres which gives its name to a brand of beer and Cape St Vincent, that is Portugal's lands end.

After a boring hour's drive, Sagres was if anything more boring. We drove on and found a simple market selling tourist stuff close to the fort that overlooks the end of the land; next stop, America.

But we managed to spend an hour looking at the views and the funny hats and cane donkeys.

"Hungry? It is lunchtime."

"No," I answered, "but I do feel sticky. Can we go for a swim?"

"I am sure there are beaches and we will find one."

Sagres was improving and we spent a lazy afternoon sunbathing and paddling. The only negative were a few local lads who were playing football on the beach and kept kicking the ball in our direction, mainly because the wind was a blowing our way.

One time I kicked it back to them and being a girl miss kicked completely and it went skyward, the wind took it and it went over a small cliff and out of sight. The largest of the lads was not amused and came right up to me in a threatening manner. He towered over me and I was frightened he was about to thump me when Tony trod on his foot and pushed between us.

The lad nearly fell over and took a half swing, but it just made him totter backward. He turned on his heel and swore and walked away and the lads dispersed with a few gestures in our direction.

"See, even men get PMT," made me laugh. It diffused what could have been a situation that would have led to serious conversations like 'what would you have done if he had hit me?'

So another two hours were spent in the warm sunshine, but being May, it was cooling by five. I shivered.

"Hungry?" With that smile. Totally disarming.

"Yes, but where is there to eat this early?"

"Up there, overlooking the beach." A terraced restaurant was bathed in sunshine and looked very appealing.

We went in and sat outside, had a soft drink and decided that their menu was the same as most in Portugal, simple fish and meat dishes. No gourmet dining here. Still it did seem to suit the moment; sun setting a view over the beach where we had been laying and the sea with a few lazy waves looking like it would prefer to join us for a beer.

The prawns were soaked in garlic and when Tony leant across and kissed me, he joked that he would need a load of mints before his meeting the next day. I said that I wondered who he was meeting with that he would kiss! We were so relaxed that I couldn't believe we had only known each other for under thirty-six hours. "How can this be so good so quickly?"

"Sometimes we are lucky in life." His eyes crinkled. The eyes were so soft, you could have slept on them as pillows.

The coffee was no better than the rest of the meal, simple ingredients served simply. But it did wake me up a bit. "It's dark."

"That's what happens when the sun sets." The simple banter matched the mood, comfortable and a bit lazy. "Walk along the beach before we drive back?"

I nodded and we gathered our stuff and walked off into the darkness. As we approached the end of the beach, I had the feeling I was about to be jumped on. I was wrong and right. A figure appeared from behind a rock. "We think you should pay for the ball you lost." Then from behind noises of a couple of other lads running up to cut off any escape.

So a rapid change of mood. Three strapping lads, one with a substantial bit of driftwood in his hand and two who we could not see if they had any weapons.

"Good English, so you will understand that mistakes happen and this is a mistake you are making."

"No, you pay us ten euros for the ball and we will go away." Said in a way that meant that when we see your wallet, we will beat you to a pulp and take it.

"No, you leave now and you won't get any trouble," was enough to get the big lad swinging the wood like a club. The two lads behind pushed past me and were surprised when I cracked their heads together hard enough to stun them.

Tony took a clout with the wood on the cheek, a glancing blow as he was moving forward fast and floored the big lad just by colliding with him.

One of the other lads came towards me and the other went after Tony. I got a back hand across the face while I was kicking him in the balls and Tony took another thump on the leg with the wood as he stamped on the big lad and swung an arm at the approaching one, who backed off.

The lump of wood was now being wielded by Tony and the third lad ran off; the other two decided that an even fight was not good odds and limped off after the first.

"Well, you are a surprise. I didn't know you knew that much about male anatomy."

We cautiously walked back to the car which was parked in a dark area. We were both wary in case the lads came back, but it was quiet. Tony unlocked the car and promptly fell over. I ran around and saw from the interior light that not only was his face cut, his nose was bleeding and the knee that had been hit was swollen.

"Shall we call the police and ambulance?"

"No, I don't want a fuss. If you can drive the car, then we will be fine. Can you?"

"Yes, I have driven on the wrong side of the road before." Surprising our mood must have been so good we were joking again already. "Shall I look at that knee?"

"No, it's just a good whack and it's bruised and hurts. I guess I am getting old letting a young thug like that get a shot in, even if he was laying on the ground. I don't even have anything to mop up the blood so we will just have to leak on the car."

"We?"

"Look in the mirror. That lad must have had a ring on, it has cut your face a bit."

I had not realised but there was one of those shallow scratches but it was about four inches long and blood was dripping off me onto my blouse. The adrenalin must have stopped me noticing, I slumped.

"Are you OK?"

"Yes, I am fine, I need a bath and some sleep. I am not sure about the jeep safari tomorrow though."

"If I can go to my business meeting, then you will be fine for sitting in a bumpy jeep. Look at this as a warm up!"

I started the car and with some guidance found the road and was directed back to the hotel. *It was almost as if he knew how to direct me but he had never been there before?*

I pulled into a parking space near the hotel and we took a circuitous route to avoid being seen. By this time, neither of us wanted a fuss, we felt fine but looked worse. The bruise on his knee was a red lump and his limp was hardly noticeable, our faces looked far worse and when in his suite I managed to clip his nose with my elbow, there was an explosion of blood that went all over the tiles.

We showered and once clean, looked normal, the cut on my face was a white line by now and would be the lightest of grazes.

"Well, I liked the day but I think your evening entertainment choices were a bit dubious." Tony was obviously feeling OK, probably relieved that there was so little visible damage.

"Tony, please be serious. Are you sure we should not call the police?"

"Well, I would be inclined to but you have just driven uninsured for an hour and they would probably concentrate on the crime they could prove than on one they would have to get all sorts of evidence about and one that would damage their tourist trade."

So that was the decision made. I took the hand towels and wiped up the blood I could see and threw them in the laundry basket.

"Thank you for being so understanding, I have never been mugged before. I suppose we are lucky that we didn't get knifed." Once he had said that, I did start to shudder. "Come on, let's go to bed, a cuddle will help."

We slept like logs. I knew he was off early and he kissed me and said, "I have left an alarm for 9.00 so you don't miss your safari." Those were the last words he ever said to me. I was vaguely aware of his more formal clothes and when the alarm went off, a quick shower and a coffee set me up for a fun day being bumped around in a jeep.

When I got back, the car was still where I had parked it, but I assumed that he might have been collected. I went back to the suite and then realised that I didn't have a key.

I sheepishly went down to reception and asked if I could be let in, and that was when the man in the suit that looked 'wrong' got up and asked, "Miss Davies, can you please come with me." Police car, interview room, cell!

My lawyer nodded and said, "That fits very well. It is not what the police think happened but you had better start by telling that story. It will do until we can find a more believable one."

"But it's the truth," I almost screamed.

"Sometimes the truth is not what people want to hear."

He got up and knocked the door. A uniformed policeman opened it and they exchanged a few words, the door shut. A minute later, it opened and the detective that had arrested me came in.

"So tell me your story and I will tell you mine." A slimy snake like insinuation that I would lie and he would be above reproach, because he always was.

Some bad coffee arrived and I started my story.

"That was an interesting fabrication, very clever." The accent seemed to add to the disbelief in his voice. "I will have that typed up and you will have to sign that it is your view of the events that led to the disappearance of Mr Peterson."

I had not even know his last name. I must have been a complete fool, but I still didn't know what I had been sucked into.

"Now I will tell you my story. It is very like yours but there are differences. So you sleep with this guy within a few hours of meeting. He is a good looking guy and has lots of money so you might well be able to collect some of it. I can see the attraction, give me enough and I would have slept with him."

"The morning arrives and although, he has been a bit rough and caught your face, or did that happen when you hit him? We guess that you got him to arrange the car and then when the keys arrived, you smacked him one on the head with something very hard. The pool of blood under the sofa will tell us more. If the maid had not spotted it, we would not have been alerted."

"It must have been risky carrying him to the car but we know from your antics on the dance floor that you are more than capable of carrying a man of his build. You dump him in the boot and take him to Sagres and when it gets dark, you dump him in one of the currents and his next stop would be New York if he could have swum or floated."

I was stunned. There was no pool of blood and he was never in the boot of the car.

Photographs are produced showing where the sofa would normally have been and where had been was a pool of dark stuff that I assume must be blood. The pictures of the boot of the car also had dark patches.

"I can't see how you managed to get the drop on him though? One smack on the head might make him groggy but it would not kill him."

The door opened and a young woman brought in a file. The detective opened it and spent a good five minutes reading. All I could do was squirm, but I think that is what he wanted.

"Do you know what Rohypnol is?"

"Yes, it's the date rape drug of choice for weirdos who can't get a girl any other way."

"Well, in this case it's the choice of the girl it seems. Enough in his bloodstream to stop him knowing night and day. If you had asked nicely, he would probably have tilted his head sideways for you to hit! The blood in the boot matches and we can only assume that it is not yours. What type are you?"

"O."

"Correct, that is the other blood type we found on the sheets, where he got rough with you and on the blouse in the basket in the room. The other blood is 'A' plus the additive. What we can't work out is where you got the stuff from."

"I didn't have any Rohypnol," I screamed. "Why would I?"

"Ah, I understand now, it was his drug, you found it and fed it back to him. That was clever. I assume that you didn't need it to be persuaded, you were all over each other when you were dancing so I guess you were a very willing partner." The way the detective looked me up and down made me shudder.

I sat back, my head was spinning and I didn't have any answers for them. Everything they said was plausible and possible, just wrong.

"Are you looking at the airports in case he leaves."

"Why would we? We have enough blood to convince us that he was disabled. Do you realise that we found nearly a pint of blood in the room and the car boot. That is a great deal for a man to lose."

"How do you know it is his blood?"

"It matches traces on a man's razor in the bathroom. When the DNA comes back, we are certain it will be his. Now why don't you make this easier and agree what you did, sign a statement and we can all rest more easily. You are going to be in a jail for a long time so you need to get acclimatised, young lady," he said, using a stern warning tone now.

"No, I am innocent. I am not going to sign a lie."

"OK we will type up both versions. You can sign yours and we will continue to gather evidence until we are ready to go to court."

They took me back to my cell. I was feeling pretty disorientated and stunned that the events could be so misread. I couldn't understand the blood, that was the only thing that was a complete surprise. Why was there so much. Was I being used as a fall guy for something? My head just spun.

I climbed into the bunk and lay there stunned and shaking. Even I could see I looked guilty.

Tony's Story

Christ, I can't believe I just managed to get away with that. I have just used a false passport and got back into England. Mind you, I had to use a false one to go to Portugal, the same passport I have had for the last five years.

Actually, it's a perfectly good passport, well they both are. Real people, just not me, both I think are in mental institutions, same age and similar features, applied for properly.

I have been living here in the UK for five years, working hard, but always knowing I might get that call. Now I will have to go back home. Still, I will have enough money to buy nice home and live a quiet comfortable life as long as I do a bit of work, but even that is taken care of.

Six years ago, when the garage I worked at closed, I thought I was lost. This was the only work I knew. I was thirty and when Ivan told me he was closing the business because he was dying, my world fell apart. But Ivan came through with a plan for me. I had always wondered how a small garage in a small town in Latvia kept going.

No communist subsidies just proper commercial work. We mended cars, tractors, combine harvesters, trailers even. But then started doing small repairs on some very exotic cars. This is where I got the computer training. Ivan could not use any modern diagnostic stuff. He was magic with everything that we had through that was ten or more years old, but electronics, no.

I got a Saturday job at the garage because my dad and Ivan drank together. I washed cars, tidied up. Threw stuff in the metal recycle bin, the source of a lot of our spare parts I later discovered.

Then one day, Ivan started swearing loudly and I went over. He was cursing, "This red devil that only tells lies." A plastic box that he had connected to the car and he was pressing, well hitting, buttons and the display was showing characters and symbols constantly changing because of Ivan's flying fingers.

"Make coffee," he yelled at me. I stood back; this looked like fun, like the video games I had read about but we never could afford in rural Latvia.

"Ivan," I said, "would you like me to look at it? I am the best boy in the school on the computer." Yes, we had one computer in the whole school. I had even managed to write a program in a language called 'Basic' which helped us all with our maths homework.

Ivan looked at me blackly and stomped off muttering but didn't say no. So I did what I always did at school when there was a problem. I switched the box off.

When I switched it back on, the display said 'wait'. I could imagine this is where Ivan would start hitting keys. He hated to wait for anything. When the magic box finally stopped waiting, it said that the car was a Volkswagen Golf and asked for the engine code. I went under the bonnet and made a note, typed it in and as if by magic, I could see all the functions of the car. "What is the problem," I yelled as Ivan came out of the office with his filthy coffee mug.

"The engine light won't go out and it stalls all the time." I pressed the number that was beside engine on the screen and another screen came up. 'Display fault codes' seemed like a good idea and the machine displayed a number. I pressed the return key again and it said 'air flow meter sensor faulty'.

I yelled at Ivan, "It's the air flow meter sensor." He came over and mumbled something, took out a workshop manual and shuffled under the bonnet. He located the part and held it up, "Looks OK to me."

"Try it on that one over there." We had an almost identical car. I was flashed a very dirty look; the car wash boy telling the boss what to do, but Ivan wanted to get down the pub with my dad. It was nearly lunchtime and it was Saturday and the football started soon.

Ivan puts the part in the other car and tries it. The engine light comes on and the car stalls. He brings the part from the other car and puts it in. "What next?" He asks. I press the return key on the display. There is a display that says 'remember fault' and another that says 'part replaced'. I put in the number beside that one. The machine bleeps and says 'reset fault lights' and I press 'yes'.

The magic machine is unplugged and Ivan tries the engine. After a slight flutter, it starts and runs smoothly, no fault light.

"Can I swoop the parts back, then you can order a new one on Monday?" I ask.

"No, don't bother that car," the one that has just been robbed, "that belongs to Mrs Ozols and she can't drive and stalls all the time, plus she is thick so she won't notice the fault light."

I blush a little at his cunning. But you have to admire his nerve!

That was the start of my career as a mechanic. Once the local garages heard that Ivan could sort out problems on new cars, they all came here, strangely always at the end of the week. My Saturday job was now to use the diagnostic computer to find the problem, just read out the display to Ivan who would make notes and charge the other garage. Soon there was a new car washer.

Then I started getting notes at home. I could drop in on my way back from college (I was now seventeen) and as soon as I finished my exams, I had a full-time job.

Actually, I have to admit that Ivan then started turning me into a proper mechanic. He taught me how to do all the jobs you might have to do, even rebuilding engines and gearboxes. I was happy, employed, which was not guaranteed in Latvia, and making good money.

I had offers from other garages, but Ivan knew when he had a good thing and he gave me a bonus for all the work I did on other garages cars. He seemed to think that I was being paid for, as he saw it, my magical abilities.

Then one day there it was a six month old Mercedes! "It won't start." Well, I had to get a clean pair of overalls and open a pack of seat covers for this one, not like the usual run of the mill VW's and Fords that we normally got.

The magic computer told me the flywheel sensor was not working, so I wrote this out and gave the note to Ivan who would then call the garage. "No order one and fit it please, we have to try and get that done today." I nervously rang the local Mercedes dealer and arranged to pay the extra for delivery just after lunch.

I was very nervous. This car was worth more than all the stuff I normally worked on in a month. What if I was wrong, the box was not infallible. Lunch was chewed but hardly swallowed, it stuck. I was just nineteen and was probably about to lose my job if I was wrong.

Well, it worked. At about 4.30, a guy in dark glasses and a nice suit arrived and I had literally just driven (very carefully) the car outside. He looked at me like I was something he would rather not be involved with. "So what was it or did it start on its own again?" It was meant as an insult to what he obviously thought a child.

I replied felling affronted, "Flywheel sensor; not easy to find but we got it in the end." It was probably the most clipped sentence I had ever said.

Mr sharp suit went inside and spent some time in the office with Ivan. A bottle was produced from the bottom of the filing cabinet. No paperwork you understand, just spanners and bits and pieces but it was the office.

When he came out, Ivan came over. "Well done, Tony. We will be getting lots more like that." He tucked a note in my top pocket, it was more than a day's wages.

"What is that for?"

"It's your half of the tip he gave us, on top of the overcharge I made. Now quietly, lad, we should never have touched that car but they can't take it to the dealer because it came into the country by a bit of a circuitous route; not illegal, but close." He had seen the look on my face.

"So we will be seeing more of these. They are owned by the people who matter and have more money than sense. Well done!" He kissed me on the forehead and then regretted the taste of the brake fluid that had dripped there earlier.

I understand the process now, I didn't then. People love their cars, it is the most potent status symbol because everyone can see them in it. A house can't move, but a car that costs as much as a house is a symbol. In Latvia at that time, it said 'don't mess with me because I know the right people and I can crush you'.

So the people who 'arranged' the cars had power over the people who had the power. The best thing was that the guys who arranged the cars could keep a low profile and actually became more powerful because they had money and contacts and were not actually breaking the law, leaning heavily, but also it was not immoral.

The immorality was their client's prerogative, they were the politicians who could be bought and the drug dealers and the guys running prostitutes, so it was a barely legal business based on illegal businesses. Now I was part of it though I didn't realise it at the time. I just got on and fixed the cars, about one every week but always some extra money.

Time went by and the 'guys' we dealt with all knew that I did the work but never tried to get me to work on the side. Ivan was a good front for them, and because he paid me well for me too. I had dreamed of owning one of the cars I used to drive so gingerly, one scratch would probably have got me a beating. I did hear that was why we were doing the work, one scratch, one beating and the 'guys' needed a new garage to use.

One day, Ivan went out and when he came back, he looked grey. He was very quiet for the rest of the day and I was just about to wash the cups, as it was time to go home, when he called me into the office.

I knew there was a serious problem when he produced 'the bottle', took a swig and tipped some into the cold coffee that was in my cup.

"I have a serious problem, not a cancer but still something that can't be cured. I am going to sell up and try and have a couple of years before I go."

Ivan told the 'guys' the bad news and asked if somehow I could be kept on. So a meeting was arranged, I was to go to Riga where all the cars passed through. I spent a day getting my hands clean and buying a suit.

I was picked up by one of the drivers who told me what was expected. If I played my cards right, I could expect that I would get to stay on. 'They' would buy the garage and I would be manager. That is what Ivan thought he had arranged.

We arrived at a car showroom which had some of the cars I had worked on, I recognised three at least. So this is where they ended up after the crooks who drove them moved on to a newer model. I was told to go in and wait.

After a few minutes, someone came in the front door and I got up, assuming that this was the person who was interviewing me. I strode over and shook his hand. He said, "If you could choose a car which one and why?"

I was a little baffled, but pointed to the BMW saying, "I drove that one and it's got a manual gearbox. I liked that it's more fun than the others, they are automatic. If you are a driver, then you would buy that one!"

At that moment, a back door opened and a very stern looking man appeared, looked across at us and gave me a look that scared me half to death. He almost ran over and grabbed the other guy by the arm and guided him away, giving me another stare of pure evil. I was terrified just by the look.

The first guy stopped being led and walked back to the BMW and said, "What deal can you give me on this then?" The devil man instantly changed, his shoulders relaxed and he smiled.

"What finally got you to decide?"

"Your new sales guy, he gave me a reason to buy the BMW."

"My new…oh yes, Tony. He is just here on trial for a day." A smile in my direction that was much less cold but still said KEEP QUIET. So I did. I went and sat down and picked up a brochure, actually it was a price list. Even these older cars were being sold for a year or two's wages!

The buyer was walked to an office and a phone call was made. A girl came out of the back door and came over. "Tony, can you come out the back please." This was in earshot of the buyer and was delivered with a lovely smile which did in part calm my nerves.

I heard the hard man say, "Excuse me for a minute," and he followed us through the door. His expression changed as soon as the door had closed. Then he reached for my head and gripped me in a vice like grip. It hurt like hell, my head was being crushed and dragged towards him.

Then he kissed me! Let me go and said, "You sit down there." To the girl he said, "Get him coffee and cake. I will be an hour with this."

He strode out the door, the girl came over. "You must have done something right. I have never seen him treat someone new like that. Do you take sugar and milk?"

The hour was spent talking to Alise who was the secretary and general dogsbody, but she did know everything. She also knew who I was from my reputation. I discovered I had been kissed by George who was the second in command and actually did most of the running of the place. All too soon he came back.

"Thank you, I have been trying to get that man to buy for six weeks and no one wanted that BMW because it was not an automatic. You must have an honest face. Now what shall we use you for?"

"I thought I was going to stay as your mechanic. Are you not going to buy Ivan's?"

"No, we are not, we can't leave any traceability. Ivan will be paid, but to keep quiet. We do look after people who are good and we have known about you virtually since you started fixing things for us, but no one here had ever met you. You are better educated and speak well, we expected a peasant with a few brains."

"You," he stood back, "could pass as a car salesman. I think I can convince the boss to use you in something much cleaner and better paid than being a mechanic in the middle of nowhere!"

From then on, I didn't look back. My parents had moved away and I rarely saw them, I had no ties except the garage and that was gone. I worked first managing the cars as they arrived, looking them over and assessing any problems. I did sometimes use a much better computer to diagnose a problem, but I wore a suit and a mechanic would take the car away and fix it taking orders from me. It felt good!

About a year later, I had a flat, a part-time girlfriend, and my English was much better as I handled the transportation of cars that were brought in from the UK and shipped there as we were a supply line from Germany. It seems that Latvia was a bit of a hub, avoiding the traditional supply routes and blurring cars true identity. I was dealing with about twenty a month in both directions.

New ones being shipped to the UK as 'low mileage' so they didn't attract as much tax. Then the true mileage would be reinstated in the computer and they could be sold as 'virtually new', but a drug dealer or a pimp does not worry quite as much as a managing director! We used to get back new cars that had been bought, the tax reclaimed, and after a year in a very clean store were brought here again with virtually no tax to pay.

One day, there was a problem and the boss told me I had to go to England and sort it out. "I can't, I don't have a passport." He hauled me to my feet. He could be very physical and I had heard, hurt a lot of people but didn't seem to mind me.

"Sit don't smile, neutral expression." I obeyed. The camera clicked.

He disappeared and I went back to work. An hour later, he was back and he handed me a brown envelope. In it was a plane ticket, and two passports, one Latvian and one UK, both with my picture one with my name and the other with my first name, but a different surname, an English one.

"Use the Latvian one, it's perfectly legal. I took the liberty of using your signature from one of the company forms."

So I left the country for the first time. The problem was not actually a problem, just poor communication and face to face it was sorted in ten minutes. A long way for ten minutes.

Gary, the English contact, and I were talking on the way back to the airport. "With your English, you could almost pass for one of us." He was only partly joking as we had been through what I discovered was typical of the English. They would declare prejudice, be open and honest and the brand you as a stereotype, then call you that to your face 'not a typical Polak sponger'.

I was already Tony the Polak. I tried twice to tell them I was Latvian before I was told it was not an insult, but actually an indication that I was accepted. I had learned an important lesson in irony.

Two months later and I was living in England, making sure that there were no more communication problems, doing the same job but in a different country. I was also being paid more, with the promise that if a particular opportunity, that scared me witless, came up I would never have to worry again. I would have enough money for a house in Latvia and enough so I didn't have to work too hard ever again. Not that this was anywhere near as hard as Ivan's garage!

There I was living a comparatively high life for someone who a generation ago would have been a Latvian peasant, boiling up scraps of vegetables for soup. I had money, nice flat, good clothes and with them came the opportunity to meet, to put it politely, girls. I liked the English girls; they were clean, they use deodorant and razors, had good teeth, not like the poor dentistry where I came from.

I was lucky that I got a toothbrush for my fifth birthday! My life was about as good as it could get, even if it meant being involved with a 'slightly' illegal business.

Then I get the call, I say I don't want to do it, I get reminded that I have passports that are 'dubious' and I will be back home with no job in twenty-four hours if they make a call. OK, I say what do I have to do?

Nothing illegal I am told. Next day, a younger version of me arrives and I brief him on how to do my job. A week later, I am in the clinic in London.

The nurse says, "So you are off to Africa? I would love to go, but not the nasty area you are off to!"

"Yes," I say, "so let's hurry up and get this blood taken so I can get my flight tomorrow." I get a vaguely dirty look but for the money that is being for paid a professional service, it can be ignored. "Just lay down and I will be back in forty-five minutes, we are waiting for the special sterilised bags to be couriered."

I was warned this would happen, it actually was part of the plan. When the door closes behind her, I take out my hip flask and drain it. If I ever get given this blood, it will make me pretty woozy if the effects that I am feeling come back with the blood!

In she comes and I can hardly raise my head. I have been given a script that I am following but she does not know this. "I am scared of needles so please don't let me see!" I plead. This hides the side effect of the drug.

An hour later, I am using the same excuse that I feel awful because of the fear of needles and sight of blood to hide my woozy feeling despite having taken the Romazicon to counter the effect of the Rohypnol.

I somehow get downstairs to the waiting room where I am joined by my 'driver' who very efficiently takes the blood in its special container and makes the joke about selling it once he gets it to Africa to make money as it is clean, not like theirs.

I sign the bill which is over £1000 just to take a pint of blood. I do see who the bill is going to, but immediately forget because it will be better for me if I don't know.

Now, I did lie about the next day departure. I spend a week in a hotel just doing nothing. Then on the Wednesday, I get the call. "Be at Gatwick tomorrow for the 12.50 flight to Faro. Your ticket will be with you in an hour." Click.

So I get up in the morning, pack, have breakfast and head off for Gatwick. I have had a week to read the brief of what I am supposed to do. I don't believe it and I don't believe that I can do it but the thought of that muddy cold Latvian village that I used to call home keeps me focused.

I see her first sitting in the bar being ogled and leered at by a pack of four lads and wonder if I am meant to be a bodyguard as well? So now I know what she looks like in the flesh. Actually, quite a nice amount of quality flesh showing, not too much but enough to inflame lads who are probably on their fourth pint since arriving thirty minutes ago and are 'on holiday now'!

I carefully rip up the photograph I have and put in three different bins as instructed. I can see that our flight has been put on the board but she shows no sign of moving. What if she is on another flight, or misses this one? No one has given me a plan 'B' and I don't have a phone number now since they took my mobile from me and gave me this new one.

Thank heavens, she drains her glass, so do the lads, they follow her out. What if they start getting heavy? I follow about thirty metres behind, but always behind other people. Another thank you god, the lads are queuing behind a flustered mother and whining child they are off to Amsterdam. I wonder what for?

My quarry slows and gets through the gate and sits facing me as I queue. She is looking at me! Does she know? Is this some sort of set up and I am the mark! I think about running but instead give my boarding card and passport to the girl. I realise my panic has been misinterpreted as being aloof and I crack a weak joke. Wow I must be doing something right, she almost screams with laughter.

Now, past the ditzy ticket dolly, don't look at her, no don't look at the blonde with the inflated chest either; oh bugger now I have given her ideas. I must admit they are a particularly well presented set though. Actually, just my type, obviously easily available! But back to business and there is a seat beside my target. "Excuse me, can I sit here?"

Naomi's Story

I always knew that he cheated. Well, he cheated on his wife with me so I could not be surprised, could I!

It's not that I don't care; as long as I get the trappings it is fine. I don't want to know and I don't want my nose rubbed in it. I suppose that is why I did what I did. Cruel really. I bet he is wondering why she never came back. Well, he won't be wondering long, I think it is going to be in the papers soon. I hope it says 'Tart kills lover'.

He will never miss the £200K it cost either. I have been taking an extra ten most months since we got our joint account and we have been married for eight years now.

I wonder how they did it? How can you arrange for someone to disappear. God I hope they didn't lie to me and actually had him killed.

That Detective Steve Morris charged me £3,000 to just get the background and another £1,000 to pass me a mobile phone. God knows how he knew who to call, but I suspect there is a network of bad guys just like builders, one will know who to call for the next type of 'service'.

Too late to worry now and if it all goes wrong, I will say it was Carl's idea! I will say I confronted the potential father of our children and he agreed to sort it out so she could never hurt us again. Why does he feel the need to have these young women? I am willing and I think very able to satisfy the needs of a man. The only explanation is he is one of those men who need extra variety. Who knows, maybe this will clip his wings for a while.

In many ways, it is his fault that I caught him. Mentioning that the gym wanted some new promotional brochures. Thinking that I was too meek to actually call the owner and getting the brief. That was supposed to be his surprise. I was going to turn up and take his photograph at the gym, but instead ended up with a picture of him holding her rather tenderly, half-hidden behind the weights rack.

I ran. I literally ran away. I phoned and said I had been called to my mother and would come back tomorrow.

There I was standing on the pavement, shaking, worrying that he might see me through the glass and there he was still gently rubbing her upper arm. You could not see who it was now but they were still there oblivious to everyone.

I wanted to hurt him so much then, but I didn't dare in case he retaliated. With his money, he could have had me 'disposed of', he was certainly ruthless enough. So I went ahead with the assignment. But did pay special attention to the picture of 'her'. Now I knew what she looked like, it was easy to get another shot of her on the running machine. Not too good a picture you understand one that would be rejected.

I did get all the names from the records of the members who I had photographed. "Just for the record so they can be contacted for approval to use the pictures."

Going over them with the owner, we put together an excellent new brochure and when Carl saw it, he was over the moon at how well I had done. "No pictures of me then?"

"No, darling. I don't think I even saw you in there. Are you sure you actually go or is the membership just for show." Laughter and a genuine sense of fun in his eyes, perhaps I also saw a tinge of relief.

Once that was out of the way, I started plotting; first a private detective. One from miles away who would have no idea who he was following.

I remember him being so greasy and having a non-descript green car. I suppose that was the only way he could function, by being almost invisible.

"Well, Mrs Molinero, your husband has been being a rather naughty boy. Every Tuesday and Thursday lunchtime he spends with the young lady, the one you gave me the picture of. There is no doubt I do have actual pictures and I expect you will need them for your solicitor. My report is here so if you could see your way clear to paying the balance for the assignment."

The last word was left like someone stranded after the last train has left a station, it was said dejectedly and sadly. Another sad tale to repeat to mates at his pub. Perhaps pictures that would be used to spice up his sex life. I shuddered at the thought of him having sex.

"No, I need you to do more. I want a complete report on this woman. I want to find a way to stop her seeing my husband and I want a way to hurt her."

"Well, Mrs, that will of course cost a little more than we originally agreed. I think about…"

I cut him short and said, "Double should do it. How much harm can I get for that?"

"I am sorry, Mrs, I can't really harm her. It's illegal and I don't think I would like prison food."

"OK then get me the information, but only if you know someone who will do the harming for me. Someone who will never implicate me and will never get caught." I suspected it would be the man on man sex in prison that really frightened him!

So a week later, I have an envelope with a full overview of another person's life. Where she banks and shops, she is a freelancer working for several companies. At the bottom is a mobile phone and a mobile phone number.

"There you go, Mrs, one personal profile, one contact number as requested now can I have some money please." I give him a cheque and he gives me an invoice, all legal and above board as he claimed to be.

"Now, Mrs, when you phone that number you will not need to say very much, keep it very simple. You can say 'a broken arm will cost how much to set' and they will tell you. They already have this report and that number is a pay as you go mobile especially for you. That way they can't get confused, that would be dangerous."

He gets out of my car. I wonder if the valet company could do a quick clean, it seems very dirty in here. I feel frightened. Then a photograph falls out, one of her going into a building.

"Good morning, I understand that you have some sort of problem you need solving?" A very quiet confident voice. Like the AA.

"Yes, I need a package put away for at least ten years."

Private Detective Steve Morris' Story

Money for old rope! As long as men have a dick, there will always be some who stray, as long as that happens there will be work for me to watch them and report back about what, or perhaps more accurately who, they have been 'up' to.

That Naomi paid an extra grand to have the introduction and the guys who will do the dirty work will pay me the same.

The only guy I have to deal with is poor old Mark, my old school buddy, who got knocked over when he was drunk one night and because he was only sixteen, no one seemed to care. He can get out of the wheelchair but honestly how do people expect him to cope with life on the legal side of the street.

He was lucky that his uncle Bob knew the guy who sets up the 'Behind the Bike Sheds' vaping franchise and felt sorry for him. I suspect Mark's uncle Bob was behind the years free rent that helped it get established, but only because the guy who owned it owed money to the local 'lord'. Funny how here in South London, we still have a feudal system with a lord in charge of the other, or shall we say, dark side of commercial activity.

Mark does not fence any stolen goods, just sells dodgy vape and happens to know everyone. Funny, a few years back, there were gangs who you would not meddle with, now the 'lord' has a couple of helpers and the rest is sub contracted! Just like most work these days.

Still on now to the next job. This will be more interesting as it's the husband who thinks the wife is playing away and she is stacked! A few pictures of her will get the guys in the pub laughing when they see the bloke, he must be rich to have bought her. One of the best looking wallet walkers I have seen in a while she is.

Naomi's Story

The voice on the end of the phone said, "Ten years is difficult, not impossible, but expensive. You have to kill someone to guarantee ten years."

He must have heard the sharp intake of breath and added, "No one actually gets killed, it just looks like it."

God, what am I doing? I look at the woman's picture; slim, athletic, confident and I look up and see my face in the car mirror. I am short, a bit overweight and I can see I need my upper lip threading again!

"How expensive?" I ask.

There is a pause. "I will call you back in less than five minutes; if you don't answer instantly then we will never speak again." The phone clicks off.

I wait trembling and staring at the mobile. It is a cheap handset. I notice the battery is fully charged, plus there is full signal; this for some reason gives me some relief. I guess it is the normality of it against this surreal situation I have created.

The handset vibrates and I nearly throw it out of the window. There is 'no number' but I press the green phone symbol and say 'hello', almost formal. I am shaking and feel sick.

"Two hundred thousand pounds, twenty before we start to set it up, eighty before we press the go button and one hundred when it's done. If you don't come up with the last payment, we implicate you and you go to jail." There is a pause then, "You need to agree or not now. If you do, then we proceed if not then this never happened." Another pause. "You have thirty seconds before I hang up."

I look in the mirror. "How do I pay you? Not in cash I hope."

"You will get a text with a particular eBay auction for a car. It is well over priced but you will 'buy it now'. Future payments will be arranged in a similar way. If you are ever caught, you can explain how you bought ten cars but never got them!"

"Agreed." The phone clicks and I look at it. What am I supposed to do now? Wait, go, what? The phone beeps. It is a text!

'Turn the phone off for twenty-four hours. Within forty-eight hours, your set up instructions will be sent by text'. Almost like a service message again from 'no number'. I turn the phone off and start the car.

At home, Carl arrives from work. It is a Tuesday so I am expecting him to be happy as he will have seen 'her'. He is relaxed it seems.

A playful smack on the bottom that stings. "Ow that hurt!"

"You know I love your bum." He is fondling now. "Soft and sweet and squeezable." Inside I am reviled and want to pull away. I realise that he is often like this after he has been with 'her'. I can't react so I have to pretend and purr.

"Well, you had better take it out to dinner then."

"Great idea, then you can show me the pictures you have done for the gym. They told me you got the job, well done! When you get paid, you can take me out as commission!"

I get drunk and compliant as I know what is coming. I can't get the picture of her out of my head and I wonder if the lies he tells me about my body, when he wants sex, he uses in reverse on her.

The next two days, before the text arrives, are like a bad dream. I function on automatic pilot. It is like having a bad cold, you don't feel like doing anything, but you function—wake, wash, dress, cook and yet when there is nothing to do, I just sit and stare into space.

I feel so detached now and go through the process. I switch the mobile off and on as requested. Always the text is waiting for me when I switch on. 'Your criteria for a car has been found go to'; then an eBay web address where a car is portrayed.

I 'buy' the first one and am told to wait two weeks. Then again another two weeks with 'be patient' added. Then after six weeks, I get another car to buy. As soon as that is paid for, another text arrives and I 'buy' all four cars even being told what to leave as feedback.

That time was the strangest time in my life. I was producing the gym's brochure, dealing with graphic designers, photographers for general views and printers all sorts of 'stuff', and as well I had my 'other' job—semi-professional hard woman and part time cuckolded wife.

One Tuesday, Carl comes back in a foul temper and I wonder. I switch the mobile on for my two weekly update and, coldly, am told to buy five more cars at £20,000 each.

The balancing act of the next week nearly breaks me mentally. I have to pay out the £100,000 knowing that if I don't, I will be in trouble, yet regretting what I am doing and wishing I could turn back time.

A last text arrives telling me to cut up the sim card and dispose of the phone where it will be destroyed. I put it under the wheel of my car and drive over it. The bits go into various local bins. I feel cold, empty and have an all-consuming guilt. What have I done. Carl is being cold and I am as well.

One night, I drink too much wine and as we are lying in bed, I roll over and cling to him. At first, he is stiff and unyielding then slowly he melts. We make love, rather than rutting, for the first time in ages, maybe years.

I wake early the next day and wonder how all this is going to happen. Who is there around who will do these things?

Mark (the Vape) Story

Feeling really cheerful today; the sun is shining and I have a decent job to plan and oversee. My old school mate, Steve, has come up with a cracker. He normally has two a year but has been quiet. He knows where I work and could have dropped past but I think he prefers not to be seen in my 'den'.

I can't 'do' anything myself but I am like a bookie. I lay off the jobs like they lay off bets. I can choose the best guy or guys to suit.

My uncle Bob runs the heavies and that helps with my burner phone sales!

Now this job is interesting because Bob has to find someone to 'die', or rather pretend to. It's quite simple with the right connections. There are lots of people in the UK who are not quite 'right', brought in to work and have a good life but can be used as cannon fodder for the right scam.

Usually, they are looked after well and when they go back to where they come from they tend to be much better off. Its rags to riches for them and only the tax man suffers!

Even the phone call made me smile!

"Hello there, I am looking for Mark, the guy who gets things done!"

"That's me, Steve. My new phone number making you nervous? What do you need?"

"Mark, you bastard, it's been a year since I have needed your 'services' so I had to go through god knows how many low lifers to find you again."

"Well, I am hardly going to advertise am I. I do have a kettle and tea bags should you decide to come back to your roots, or should I say back down to your roots! So stop being so snooty and from now send a text every month, then when I get a new phone, which I do every year, I can let you know. I always have a one month overlap so I can keep the people I want and dump the ones I don't."

"Mark are you still running that vape shop?"

"Yes, I am. How do you expect a poor lad in a wheelchair to make ends meet?"

"From all the people who come to you to get their 'issues' sorted. Apart from me, you must have fifty blokes and tarts who will collect debts and whatever else you want them to? Funny how nowadays you need almost as many tarts and blokes. I hear you have some lookers too. Can't be all bad?"

"No, but 'the ladies' are not interested in me except for their burner phones and the 'special' vape I sell, quite new but very easy to sell and the cops can't yet tell one sort from the dodgy stuff; no spliffs or even the smell; good margins too."

"You clever bastard. I will slum it and drop in and see you soon. I could do with a bit of undetectable puff. Helps wind down after a job."

"So, Steve, drop by. I can't go far as you know. So what are you after anyway?"

"I have a client who is asking for her husband's tart to be 'put away' for ten years."

"Well, Steve, that will be a retail price of 200K and we will have to pay that private dick who makes the connection 1K out of that. Does that suit you?"

"Yes, Mark, no problem."

Mark calls his uncle Bob.

"Bob, its Mark. We have a job to organise; 200K less one for the private dick who brought it to us."

"OK, Mark, there will be ten in it for you. Send her a mobile and when you hear from her, get the details and I will drop in and get them."

Well, as you can imagine that makes me very happy, a decent job to plan and oversee. I do get so bored just running a shop and the 'plan' is only ever written down like a story as if I write short stories. If the cops ever come after me, I have twenty that are in my cupboard and I doubt they will ever be clever enough to realise that they are actual facts not fiction!

That private dick, Steve, comes up with jobs, usually two a year, but this is the biggest so far. It's usually a roughing up with one decent kick in the balls to put the straying guy off sex for a while.

This job will be difficult. I have Uncle Bob who will provide the basic manpower. It's no problem for him. He will get some of my wedge and if anything goes wrong, he will be the trouble-shooter. He will take the job over and although, I will get less, there will be no comeback.

So the first thing I need from Bob is someone who will be the patsy who 'dies'. I know Bob has the contacts who have 'staff' who are over here, in shall we say not quite legal status, working, paying tax; proper people who can be relied upon to do what is asked. They get a good pay-out and have in any case have to be moved on at regular intervals so no one tries to dig too deep into who they are.

Basically, they are people who can be controlled with money and coercion, not slaves in the broad sense, but people who have accepted that they will do as they are told in return for a much better life than they had in whatever previous existence they had and will as well take on a task that may put them in some danger but it will be worth their while.

Once they complete their task, they have a bit of a 'rags to riches' change which makes them happy and keeps them quiet too. The tax man might suffer at that point but we all feel so sad about that.

Carl's Story

I am so stupid! Why did I tell that ditzy wife of mine about the gym needing a new brochure. I know it won't make any difference because the chances that she will even try to get the job are pretty low. Still, I will warn Jane next time we meet up. No more quick meetings behind the weights' rack.

I should have told her yesterday but forgot. She has such a cheeky way with her I was distracted. Fancy lifting her top like that, luckily no one saw. One day, I will decide if I prefer large or small boobs, but for the moment, I am happy having both. Jane, the gym bunny, is so different to Naomi, the housewife. They are complete opposites which I suppose is the attraction, variety being the spice of life.

I will tell Jane next week at the hotel. She will give me a hard time but I know she is no saint so it won't be a problem. It is a shame I can't call her in case the wife sees the number. I must get a cheap phone so we can contact each other more easily. We are not in love but we are very much in lust!

I would call her mobile but that means records that Naomi might see. My mobile bill is on line but I have to print it out for the tax man and I am too careful for that. Only the police are going to trace text messages but I can't really put something this delicate in a text as they are so easily misinterpreted.

So all the loose ends tied up, I think, tracks covered and I don't need to worry.

***

Pissed off does not even come close. I have been waiting in this tatty hotel room for two hours and she has not shown. No text and her phone is off. Jane has always been so enthusiastic and reliable; always lets me know if she was going to be a bit late in plenty of time.

Sod it. I will have to go back to work and sort out that shipment. That prat who messed up the container allocation is going to get his fortune told. I will enjoy ruining his day. It does not help when I remember it was the same product that Jane had been working on when I met her.

I will have to ask quietly at the gym if anyone has seen her. I know they suspect we are bonking but they can't be sure. We always leave apart if we see each other and only 'chat' when we bump into each other.

Yes, plenty to do. I have to place the trainers that are in this shipment but that should be no problem. Always plenty of takers of genuine branded trainers, all legal and above board, but made for foreign markets. Buy them directly by pretending to be in Africa and the price is so much lower. Then get them transhipped.

It's just a matter of having a direct line into the shipping company. If you give them the exact info, they don't care where it ends up. I pick up the freight cost either way.

I am glad that thick wife of mine has a bit more work now. Less chance of getting caught and she is much calmer than a few weeks ago, almost reserved. Not sure on consideration I like that. God, now I think of it, is she having an affair. Maybe she is not as thick as I thought.

Not sure I am happy about this. I can't accuse her or she could come back at me. Jane was not the first and I am sure she has some inkling. I will have to play it a bit cool and see where we go. I can't afford a divorce at the moment; there are too many 'grey' areas of my financial arrangements. I had better get them well hidden just in case.

Well, it looks like Jane may have done me a favour, possibly a clean break and a new start. Pity I like Naomi. She is cuddly, fun and easy, if you know what I mean; not too much of a challenge. Jane, like the rest of them is, or do I mean was, the challenge.

Mark the Vape

"Bob?"

"Yes, who else answers my phone?"

"That package we discussed, put away for ten years, female, thirties. Socially active as they say and a bit too much with the client's husband."

"Around the 200 mark we said with your cut in there."

"The money's deposited. Get a set up over to me so I can approve it, then I will send you the cash so you can get all the players in place."

Mark calls Bob.

"That was a sweet plan. I like the twists. Let me know when the blood has been taken, can you get a trace on her working in the meantime."

***

"Hi, it's Bob. I need a person followed and we need to know if she plans any trips away."

"OK man, no problem. Usual fee for the phone and computer tracing and a couple of followers. I think I have the leg men around and the tech guy will get into her as soon as we have a pattern to make sure her home is empty."

"It's Bob. The target has just booked to go to Portugal; Easyjet 2233 to Faro on the 17 (watch dates, etc.), staying at the Rivero in Portimao. I have arranged one watcher to go with them and we will have two over there and a car. Should be easy. We even get the Portuguese to pay for the trial and feed her no drain on our taxes."

"Neither of us pay any tax."

"Oh come on, where is your sense of humour! I forgot you don't have one when you are working. We must have a beer or twenty soon, once we have been paid."

"OK yeah, we can do that but we need to concentrate on this going perfectly. Make sure it does. All the guys reliable?"

"Yes as far as anyone can tell. The main player is from the import people but they have not let us down before."

The Television News

"Our main story tonight is that a young British woman has been arrested for murder in the Algarve in Portugal."

"Jane Adams, thirty-three, was arrested at around 5.00 pm today for the murder of Tony Peterson. Portuguese police are not giving out any other information at the moment but it is believed that the couple travelled to Portugal together on Thursday, two days ago."

"We will try and bring you more information in our late bulletin."

"In London, today the demonstration against…"

Mark the Vape

"Bob, it's Mark. That twat only got chatting to a blonde in Seville. I think a rap on the knuckles is in order. 1% fine do you think?"

"Yes, Bob, I agree. That's the trouble with some of these guys, they need a good slap before they start so the rules are obeyed. It's not bloody football where they get away with the small fouls all the time. It's like we are in the army and they are civilians; we know orders are orders, they think rules can be bent!"

"Have an eye kept on him at the hotel. Just a daily visit, but watch the checkout day. The guy will go with the driver, no contact with anyone else for any, and repeat that to him, any reason."

Tony's Story

I toss the mobile phone into the bin inside a food bag and the dismembered sim card in another.

It has been a bit of a drive here to Seville, no speeding and being extra careful, but I was told that I could not risk CCTV picking me up in Faro. It won't be long before some picture of me appears in the Portuguese papers but I don't think they will be very clear.

Ryanair to Stanstead, different airline and different UK airport.

Using my Latvian passport, the UK one cut into strips in several bins and the identification pages burnt carefully. I think I have followed the instructions.

Baseball cap pulled down and greyed hair for when I have to take it off will I am sure keep me 'hidden'.

No looking at any women and especially that blonde over there. A bit older than I would normally go for but I would not kick her out if she asked nicely.

I need a drink. There is time so a brandy and coffee slide down as did the second brandy and that helps untie the knots in my neck.

What have I done? I was not keen on that Jane but what did she do to be framed for my 'murder'?

The flight is now on the monitor and as I slide off the stool, I realise that the blonde lady has been sitting next to me and as I move so does she! God, why is it when you don't want the attention, it is there! "Sorry, I didn't see you."

"No need to apologise, it was as much my fault."

I am looking at a pair of flirty eyes and notice a cleavage that is 'interesting' below as she looks up at me. The smile says 'I have seen you and I don't mind'.

"Are you going to Stanstead too? I guess you must be as it's the only flight being called!"

Clever bitch. Still two brandies has weakened my resolve and what harm can it do at this late stage? I am not allowed to contact anyone from my past in the

UK. this 'bends' the rules I think but not really a break. OK a clear break but one that can't hurt, can it?

So a flight that was going to be uncomfortable, it's Ryanair remember, and boring is only going to be uncomfortable.

As we land, I am offered a small slip of paper with a mobile number on it. It is very tempting but I say 'no' as I am going to be 'travelling around a lot for the next couple of months', and luckily she has luggage to collect and I have left everything in Portugal; being dead I had to.

As I come out of the customs and immigration, I see a driver with dark glasses and a peaked cap and no sign. He will be mine then. As I walk up he turns and walks away. That is the signal.

No words are exchanged and as I get in the back of the car, I find a small case. Inside are some paperwork plus a mobile. It rings.

"You didn't keep any contact with that blonde tart?"

"No, she offered but I resisted." I had not realised I was being watched! I should not be surprised though. I am sure I followed all the other rules.

"Good because you were a breath away from losing some part of your body. You don't break the rules at all. It will cost you 1% of your fee."

I sit there stunned and resentful. But totally powerless. They held all the cards and I am totally dependent on them for my future.

The phone clicks off and I sit watching the countryside from the car. I don't dare ask where we are going.

We pull off the motorway and soon into a small industrial estate that is half deserted and pull up outside a unit with 'for rent' outside. The door is open and the driver points through the door. Inside the sign says 'reception on the first floor', so I go up the stairs.

Here there is a man who is completely unidentifiable like the driver.

There are two suitcases and on a tatty desk a sheaf of papers.

I get handed a sheet of paper and one word is uttered 'read'.

Apart from your unauthorised contact on the plane, you have completed what we wanted you to do. You will hand this sheet back.

You are entitled to, and there are here;

Hotel booking for a week close to East Midlands Airport so you can do any shopping you want. You must never come back to the UK.

There is a one way booking including extra baggage ready paid for to Riga. Get a taxi to the centre of Cesis and go to the property agent near the castle, and tell them the name in your new passport. Give the old passport to the man here.

They will give you the keys to a car that is registered in your name and the keys to a small villa close by. It is leased for a year. You can buy it for a discounted price that the agent will give you. You can afford it.

After one year, if you stay in the villa, you will be contacted and different work offered.

Do not try and contact us in any way.

If you get into trouble, you can explain this in any way. All we have done is traceable back to you as 'you' have arranged it.

There is a bank account in your name details here.

There is enough cash to keep you going until you get to your villa.

I handed my passport over. The man helped me downstairs to the car and the cases were loaded into the boot.

Another quiet drive to a hotel where I unpacked my old clothes from the cases, I noticed that all the labels had been carefully removed.

I take off my jacket and realised the new phone they had given me was in the pocket. I found the slip of paper that the blonde on the plane had obviously slipped into my pocket, two numbers, landline as well; god she must be keen or desperate.

I left it on the side and started reading the hotel blurb. I would have to eat soon and needed a drink. On the bottom of the hotel brochure detailing the facilities was the address and phone number. Something familiar there, the code was the same as my blonde fan. That was a coincidence.

Well, I think I deserved a treat so I called her. You should have heard her almost drooling when I said hello!

We agreed to meet here in the hotel 'when she had got herself ready', two hours as it happens.

Well, she might have been a bit older but she made up for it with enthusiasm and as I said goodbye in the morning, I reluctantly said that I would be leaving soon on the 'travels'.

Just to be certain I change rooms explaining the 'situation' to the guy on reception who made sure I was 'checked out' in case she called. I said my wife would not understand as 'the wife' might be turning up.

Well, home free it seems. Six days to sort out any bits I might need, say goodbye to England.

I sleep all day. I had not got much the night before!

Jane's Story

It has been three more days now. I have had to repeat my story every day, apparently it's the way they find chinks in it. That is according to my greasy solicitor. The British consul has been in and said it looks bad. He looks like he would like to believe me but the blood test results are the final bit of evidence that buries me it seems.

The only thing they can't explain is why I did go on the safari and come back to the hotel. Just some vague excuse that I had left some unspecified evidence. I keep plugging away at that but they just say I was coming back because I had forgotten something and asking what it was. Unfortunately, I did have my passport and all my credit cards on me when I was arrested so I could have been fleeing.

There is no one in the UK who I can call, no really close friends and I don't have a 'proper' job so no employer to help.

The food here is disgusting but I don't feel like eating much. All I can do is pray they will find out what happened. It was someone else but the hotel CCTV shows nothing I am told and what did they do with his body?

A key in the door, it opens. "Come with me please." As we leave the cell, I am handcuffed with my hands in front of me. This is new.

I am led out but we don't turn left for the interview room. We head for a door that looks like it leads outside. We push through and I am half-blinded by the sunlight. Straight into a prison van, no one has told me where I am going!

There are no windows in the van and the seats are not padded at all, no sharp edges and simple lap seat belts. I am handcuffed to a burly policeman but at least there is a policewoman in the back of the van with us.

We stop and I wait while the door is opened from the outside. As it does, the cameras start to flash and I am pushed through the crowd up some steps and into a quiet building and into a small room.

Here sitting down is my solicitor, he looks up and smiles.

"I won't ask you how you are, but I have good news!"

My heart leaps am I going to be freed? He sees my face and scowls so I sit down demurely.

"They are not going to charge you with murder, only manslaughter. They are not happy but with no body, it is the rule. They think you are very clever as to dump him at Cape St Vincent, a masterstroke as he will be half way to New York by now."

If that's the good news, I am not feeling good. "I didn't kill him and I don't know what has happened to him." I went quiet. "What will I get as a sentence if I am found guilty?" I ask.

"Twenty years, but that will half and you will get to spend the last bit of your sentence in the UK."

Ten years; I will be in my mid-forties before I get out and what will the rest of my life be like? No, I must fight this. "What is going to happen today?"

"You will be asked your name. It will all be in Portuguese and English so you can understand." I nod. "Then you will be told the charge and if you want to plead guilty or not. You know that if you fight this, you will serve longer. If you plead guilty, then we can pretty much guarantee the twenty reduced to ten."

The door opens and two policewomen come in and take the handcuff off the desk ring and I am attached to the larger lady. They are taking no chances.

It goes as the solicitor says and I am tempted to say 'guilty' but I have to say 'not'. I can't cope with this. I want to be away from here. I want to go home.

The police oppose bail and that is agreed and I am told that there will be one month before the trial while evidence is collated and can be checked by my defence team (I am told I will also get a proper counsel as well as my greasy solicitor).

I am led away and out the back of the courthouse, and this time, we go to a prison. Here I am told that I will get some comforts as a foreign national. I am allowed some of my own clothes and shower gel but nothing much. These little things at first hearten me but soon I feel even more depressed as I can see my life shrinking by the moment. They take the keys to my flat and say they are sending them to the British police so they can search my flat for any clues or information.

I will not see my solicitor for a week and am not allowed to mix with the other 'inmates' which I suppose I am happy about.

I ask for a pen and paper and get some, so I start trying to find anything to help me. Two hours later, the paper is still blank. What is more worrying so is my mind.

Tony's Story

"George, that idiot had the blonde from the plane in his room all night. She could have looked at anything."

"OK that's enough, you can head off. We will have to deal with that. It's not bad but any more slips and we will have to deal with him. Be there on the day he goes and be ready just in case, that is six days from now. He is on the noon flight."

"OK will do. What do you need me to be ready for?"

"Up to a bad accident where a lorry crushes the car and sends it off the road."

"What about the driver?"

"Use someone illegal with no contacts. It may never happen though."

Carl's Story

I have been asking round and no one in the gym seems to know where Jane is. I don't enlighten them as she chats to the staff and none of them know about her problem yet. It was a bit of a fishing exercise. I do care about her a bit, not enough to do anything silly. It will all come out soon and I will have to pretend to be surprised.

I didn't know where she lived but managed to get that from the guy on reception. If you think girls are thick, guys can be worse. All I had to say was that I had to deliver one of the letters from my wife with a picture to be approved for the company brochure.

There is no answer to the doorbell and the door is properly locked. Nice flat in an old block. I will have to get one of my friends to get me in.

"Hi, it's Carl. You never answer this mobile, do you. I need the details of 15 New Street, Flat 9, and wonder if you can arrange for me to see round sometime."

Wonderful if you know how, it will cost £500 for a set of keys but that is cheap when you want to frighten a poor payer. My 'friend' will arrange for a bouquet of flowers (lilies usually) and a personalised card with a strong hint and that usually works. Especially, if there is a wife or girlfriend in residence.

I get the call the next day. *Great I will have the keys for later,* I think, but the next day I get a call.

"You bastard, I nearly got arrested because of you. I was just about to open the door and up the stairs come two cops with the caretaker. From what I found out later, it seems your girlfriend has a tendency for the rough stuff. She only killed a guy in Portugal three days ago. I should charge you extra but because it's you, the fee will be the same and a pair of size ten in whatever your latest scammy trainers are."

Well, I am stunned. I say thanks and hang up. Before I forget, I go to the office and transfer the money. He can stuff the trainers until he comes here.

I wander out into the late afternoon sun and think that I should have been with Jane today and didn't even cancel the hotel booking! So who did she kill and why? Yes, she was a tough cookie but tough as in resilient, not tough as in aggressive. How do I find out? Not that I owe her but I don't think anyone else is around to help her.

On my way home, I stop at the petrol station and see the headline in the paper, 'Brit Kills on the Algarve', so I buy it and sit in the car park and read all about how Jane did this guy she had just met on the plane. Some guy called Tony Peterson, a foreigner it seems, though the name sounds like a Brit.

I will do a bit of asking about him. I can't see Jane doing it; no she couldn't have. I can tell peoples' characters and she would kick you hard if you asked for it but unlike some of the guys, I know she would not enjoy it.

It seems this Tony is a bit of a car wheeler and dealer from Hertfordshire, the rich side, so should not be hard to track down.

I swing back to the office and using 192.com, do a search and bingo, up he comes. It's a few pence but very useful that.

One phone call to a local 'face' and I will get a few details in a day or two.

Home now and let's see how my lovely wife is doing.

Naomi's Story

It's 7.00 and Carl's car pulls into the drive. It's a good evening and after a glass of wine, we eat the coq au vin in the garden. He tells me about the day he has had but is far more detailed than usual. He is normally very busy but today does not seem to have as much content as usual.

I know what he does is bending the rules but it's not illegal, which is why I don't ask too many questions.

Again, he is distracted and actually helps with the plates and is loading the dishwasher and I am watching.

"Damn, I left my briefcase in the car, could you get it for me, love?"

"Of course, darling." So I go out and notice that there is a paper in the back, so I put this on top.

We are watching television and the programme ends. "Want a coffee?" I say.

"Yes please, darling. I need to do a bit of paperwork for tomorrow so can you bring it to the office? You know I hate that baking programme anyway!"

When I take him the coffee, he has the contents of the briefcase all over his desk and mumbles thanks. I look for the paper but it is nowhere to be seen which is strange, but Bake Off has started so I hurry downstairs.

An hour later, I slip upstairs and he is still working away so I look for the paper. I usually buy one but forgot. It's not upstairs anywhere and I don't want to disturb him so I go hunting downstairs.

Hall, no. Living room and dining room, no. Conservatory, no. Kitchen, no. It's just vanished.

The dishwasher has finished so I empty it, tidy the kitchen and then take out the kitchen rubbish. I am about to throw the bag in the bin and I see the paper through the yellow plastic, stuffed right down. I don't like this. What can there be to hide in a daily paper?

I take it out and read the headline, a cold shiver runs. I feel slightly faint and have to hold the fence for support. I close the bin and hide the paper in the garage until tomorrow.

Back indoors, I pour a large vodka as Carl comes in. "I thought we had enough booze with dinner," he says with a disapproving edge to his voice.

"Just a nightcap," I say. "Want one?"

"No, thanks. I have an early start so I am heading up."

I sit and drink so much that I can hardly get up the stairs but I have to force myself as he will want to know why if I fall or even make enough noise to wake him.

Next morning, I have to pretend to be OK but I am not at all. Luckily, all he does is make a quick coffee and leave. As he does that, he says, "How was that work you did for the gym? You must let me know when I am getting my commission." I look blank. "The meal, you daft woman. Tell me tonight, or better still if they have paid you, book a taxi and a table!"

The door shuts and I hear his car reverse and the gates open for him to leave.

The story is sketchy but quite clear. Man missing presumed dead, drugged, blood on hotel floor, woman assumed responsible being held. Yes, it's her. My stomach that felt bad because of the vodka now erupts and I just make it to the toilet and wretch. For minutes, I sob, wretch, sob and wretch for probably half an hour. Finally, I go back to bed and set the alarm for noon.

But who can sleep when you have caused all that misery. After an hour, I start to feel better and coffee helps. Then hunger strikes and toast helps more. I still feel 'how could I' and then I think actually I feel better. The bitch deserves it for trying to steal my husband. Now I am angry and that helps even more.

Well, as it happens, I have been paid for the brochures so I text him after booking the taxi and restaurant. I am going to enjoy a little fun here and when I go shopping, there is a follow up story with her face on the front of the paper. I drop into the restaurant and check that we have a good table and quietly leave the paper hidden in the waiting area, well enough buried that the staff won't move it.

Carl gets back early and seems chirpy enough though like he is when a deal is about to happen, as if he is waiting for something to happen. I ask and he says, "Yeah, I dropped the paperwork into the shipping company to divert a container and that's always a worry in case they lose the paperwork. We don't want those trainers ending up where they are supposed to be, do we!"

As it's a celebration, I have a bottle of bubbly ready and we toast my career. After the second glass, the taxi beeps outside and we head for the restaurant. I have deliberately booked the taxi early and the table late so we will have to have a drink first. I want him softened up.

It's a good place to eat; English with foreign influence, so you might get tapas and a good bloody genuine Angus steak, and as we peruse the menu, he downs his gin and asks for another. Perfect.

As the waiter brings the second drink, I say, "I am ready." As I actually chose what I was having earlier, Carl is flustered but chooses quickly. He does not like me being assertive.

We chat idly and then I reach for the paper that I hid earlier. "I have not seen a paper for a couple of days, what has been happening?" I plant the seed.

I lay the paper out face up on the low table and in my peripheral vision see him gulp as he sees the front page.

"She looks familiar," I say. "Where could I have seen her I wonder? She must be a complete bitch if she drugged and killed a bloke. I wonder why, not good enough in bed do you think?"

All the colour drains from Carl's face but I press on. "It says here that she will get twenty years at least and then only if it's not murder." I see out of the corner of my eye the waiter coming, so I say, "What do you think, darling, is twenty years enough?"

"Your table is ready now, would you like to follow me please."

Carl leaps up and almost runs round the table to be behind me so I can't see him. The walk to the table is just long enough for him to regain his composure which suits me fine, I want a good evening and my husband is good company. I will use the 'lucky you have me or it could have been you' another evening.

The Television News

"More information is being released by Portuguese police about the case of the man who has apparently been murdered in the Algarve."

"It seems that a body has yet to be found, just that he is missing presumed dead. The young British woman is still in police custody."

"It seems that the couple flew to Faro on Thursday on an Easyjet flight, stayed at the Rivero hotel in Portimao and were seen by several people to be well aquatinted with each other. The last that anyone saw of then was when she threw him in the swimming pool when they were dancing together. It is not clear if this was an act of aggression or not."

Carl's Story

My god that was close. I nearly threw up when the waiter arrived and distracted me. I can't say anything in case Naomi gets suspicious and she is thick in some ways but not when it comes to reading real feelings. I had just enough time to get composed and think of a joke by the time we got to the table.

I really like Jane and can't believe what is being written about her. Previous boyfriends seem to be crawling out of the woodwork and condemning her as a man eater. I suspect just because she dumped them for being too weak.

She told me that she liked strong men who are not afraid, clingy or needy and I am not. What we have, or should that be had, was initially a cheeky and fun time over an occasional lunch which one day became a challenge and a sweet sexy one at that.

Luckily, Naomi had a few drinks inside her and I rapidly added to that so she didn't belabour the subject.

Dave, the local face, says he will call tomorrow, so I will find out who this Tony is. I am not jealous, Jane can do whatever she wants and she was off on a holiday of sorts; we don't own each other. The only thing we 'promised' was that we would be serial, so no bed hopping five times a week if you take my drift.

Well, someone is snoring a treat so I am off to the spare room.

Naomi's Story

Well, that is a turn up. I had a call from a bloke called Dave who is a 'friend' of Carl's asking where he was. Must have been in a meeting with his phone on silent. Well, it seems that he has been asking about a car dealer whose name is Tony. That cannot be a coincidence as the man who was 'murdered' was called Tony and the paper mentioned the automotive trade. So that bastard husband is looking into something and I don't like it.

I have Dave's number, thanks to 1471, so I will find a way to get something extra out of him.

"Dave was trying to get hold of you earlier," I shout as Carl comes in the door. "He said you have the number."

Again, the colour drains but not as badly this time, I am enjoying this just a little bit. It serves the bastard right. He is my bastard though and I do love him. He might just stay a bit more faithful after this little episode though?

Carl heads upstairs and I hear him in his office. It's quiet for five minutes then there is a bit of thumping and bumping and he comes downstairs fast.

"Bugger, I left some papers at the office. I need to finish them tonight. Darlin', can supper wait?"

"Yes, love, no problem. It's just salad and the rest of that chicken. How long?"

"Forty five minutes, an hour tops. The traffic should be quiet." And off he goes.

The car chucks up a few stones on the way out and nearly clips the gate that is still opening.

Carl's Story

"Dave, you daft bugger, what are you doing talking to my wife?"

"Hold on there, you gave me the home number and didn't answer your mobile and I am hardly going to leave a message about that guy, am I. He disappeared and is probably dead so I don't want the cops asking to hear voicemail messages, do I?"

"OK but you had better not have told that daft cow anything!"

"No way to talk about your wife! Anyway, I don't know anything, do I. I said you were asking about a car dealer and then said that you were probably looking for a car, that not cover it!"

"OK well, you had better be quieter in future if you want paying. So what's the lowdown on this guy?"

"Well, he is a bit of an enigma. No one seems to have known him and the police have been all over his flat and it's all as if he was going on a short trip like the paper said. But what is strange is that they can't trace who he worked for and no one has a picture of him. The cops will have to use his passport photo but there is some problem with that too."

"I used a press card to ask about and one guy seemed to know him but was a bit closed. Probably didn't know anything but wanted to look big. Shall I ask any more?"

"Swing past and see if anyone in the local bars know him and let me know IN PERSON tomorrow."

"OK. That will be 300 then, OK?"

"Fine but you pay your own expenses for talking to my wife."

"You are a tight bastard, but I have another reason to be over that way tonight, so OK, I will let you know tomorrow. Hey, I nearly forgot. You owe me a trip to the horses and a few beers too. When are you paying that bill?"

"Diamond Dave, when I see you, I am going to stuff your mobile, well never mind. Yes, we must do some damage soon. You look up the next meeting and give me a couple of dates, I could do with a bit of r & r."

"Will do, Carl, take care now, and no more slagging off that lovely wife of yours. I wish mine was more like her!"

The line clicks off and I realise that I am really wound up about this. I am not sure if its Naomi, Jane or me who is the problem. I could really do with a bit of a relax with a mate like Dave so we can shoot the breeze, swear a lot and get drunk without any of the acting. It's the acting that wears you down!

The Television News

"Tonight's breaking news is that the woman arrested in Portugal for the manslaughter of Tony Pearson has been formally charged and remanded in custody. There are still few exact details, but is seems that the man may have been drugged and the dumped in the sea where local currents would wash his body far out into the Atlantic."

"British police have searched the woman's flat in London but are not giving any details. There are no details of where the man was living but it is believed that the police have searched a flat in Hertfordshire."

Mark the Vape and Uncle Bob

"We had someone asking about him today. Had a fake press card. Any ideas?"

"No, who was he really?"

"I have a mobile number and car registration."

"He needs to be mugged and his wallet and phone stolen."

"No warnings?"

"No, just as late as possible and when he has been drinking."

"How bad?"

"Nothing broken but enough bruises to slow him down. Our boy is off in four days."

"Tonight?"

"Yes."

"OK, if he shows his face again, I will arrange it."

The Television News

"More information has come to light about where the man who is suspected to have been killed on the Algarve. He may have been living in Hertfordshire. Police have searched a flat in Bishops Stortford and have been asking questions in local bars, restaurants and interviewing local residents."

"The man is now described as having a foreign demeanour, but locals always thought he was from the UK but probably with foreign parents, possibly eastern European, but some people have said he could have been Portuguese."

"I have just been told that the police are holding a news conference in the area and we have a camera crew and reporter on hand. Over to you, Simon."

"Yes, thank you. In the last few moments, police have made an appeal for any information about the missing man, Mr Tony Peterson. This is Superintendent Jones of Hertfordshire Police speaking a few moments ago."

"We have been asked by our colleagues in Portugal to assist in an enquiry regarding the disappearance of Mr Tony Peterson, although it is possible that the surname is slightly incorrect and could be a Latvian spelt Pētersons."

"Around six feet tall, athletically built. We only have a fairly poor picture of this man. He seems to have lived alone with no regular partner or visitor who was seem more than once or twice."

"He frequented local bars and restaurants but never it seems with the same person twice. We have a photofit picture and if anyone can shed any light on his life, where he worked, then that could help us and our Portuguese colleagues who as I am sure you already know are holding a young English woman who is a suspect in his disappearance."

Carl's Story

"Dave, where are you? You were supposed to get to me yesterday. What are you playing at? 300 we agreed and you didn't deliver, so unless you have a full story on that Tony and a good explanation, you can go whistle."

Mark the Vape and Uncle Bob

"Did we get the phone and wallet?"

"Yeah, no problem. So we have all the info we need, even has email on the phone, which is unusual for a thug like him."

"He was working for the guy who sells the trainers, it was his wife who employed us remember."

"We have a problem, not just the police which we expected but a privateer and he has someone who is paying him for information."

"As it's a boyfriend of the girl, is this getting a bit too close?"

"No, that is fine to be expected. Now it's all over the papers he was bound to find out and ask."

"Three days and the problem will be on a plane, he is untraceable. The papers have a full briefing from the police and they think he was doing dodgy deals on imported cars but can't find his office, but don't think it's important that it will show up at some point in the future when someone misses him. The case against the girl has enough holes to make it manslaughter but not enough to worry them. They think she is bluffing and will never give up the information."

Tony's Story

My last day in the UK. I can't say I will be sad to leave. I could never have a proper life here being here illegally. But now, I will be comparatively well off and be able to have more of a life; even a girlfriend that can last more than two dates.

Its 8.00 am and I have just had some breakfast. It's become a mini routine. Luckily, this hotel does not seem to have the same people staying more than a night or two, so no one tries to strike up a conversation. The only odd thing I notice is a guy who has been in reception for the last three days, but gone when I come out of breakfast; probably a driver for someone, or perhaps he is my 'minder'. I had not thought of that!

Well, that was boring, a whole week with nothing to do. It might be some peoples idea of fun, but I like being busy. It took a day to buy the stuff I wanted—clothes, a new iPad and things like that. I had to buy all my music again as I could not use my iCloud in case the police have the details.

I do a mental check off; enough decent clothes and shoes to last me a year. I suspect I won't be able to get anything decent in the back of beyond. They have provided the phone and I have the electronic stuff now. Enough decent shampoo, shaving gel and aftershave for a while. I think that covers all I can reasonably take.

The car will be here at 9.00 to take me to the airport so I will get on, last few things into the case and off we go.

"Hi, I am checking out, is there anything to pay?"

"Room 263, no all paid for. You didn't book anything recent to the room, did you?"

"No, I paid as I went. I don't like surprise bills."

"Well, I hope you have enjoyed your stay, Mr Schmidt. We hope to see you again soon."

"Thank you, I will stay again when I am back this way." I know I won't but I don't want any more banter.

As I turn, I realise there is someone behind me what I don't see is his fist balled up which hits me in the gut, the next one hits me on the face and my nose spurts blood. I slowly straighten up and see him pushing through the door and running away. What was that for?

The reception woman screams and staff come running. This I don't want at all. A flannel is put onto my face. Its coolness would be comforting if I was not in panic mode. My driver may be outside and he must not see anything!

Luckily, he is not yet here and I get cleaned up. The bruise is beginning to show but the blood has stopped, thank god.

"Do you want us to call the police, Sir?"

"Do you know who it was who hit you?"

"No, I have no idea, sorry and no don't bother with the police. It was probably some nutter who mistook me for someone else."

I get a cup of coffee and too much attention. I look at my watch and see it is 8.50; ten minutes, I may have just made it.

A porter is summoned to help me with my bags and he waits with me, probably under management instructions, at the front of the hotel.

"I think I know who hit you, Sir. He was talking to the senior porter one night when I came on. They came out of the security room, where all the CCTV is kept. Do you want me to find out, I will be discreet and very cheap!"

Now I am confused what does all this mean? CCTV? I can't have upset anyone, could I? Then, maybe, it clicks.

"Did you hear anything that was said?"

"Yes, something about a wife who was going to get a surprise and a guy who was not going to mess with her again."

Yes, it clicks. The blonde lady has a husband and a jealous one it seems. I wonder how he found out, she was not going to tell him. As my brain kicks into gear, I realise what happened. She did say she had a problem as the Sat Nav didn't want to work properly. He must have got in the car and found the address!

Uncle Bob and 'the Boss'

"So what happened?"

"Some random guy was waiting in reception and smacked him. Turns out, it was the blonde's husband, that was from a porter who says he has been looking at CCTV with the head porter."

"Plan B, now and quick."

"Sure."

"Sure and call me when it's all in place."

***

"All done, I had to work very fast; lucky you had it all on standby as there is no way to fake that level of accident quickly."

Tony's Story

The car arrives and I get in. Cases in the boot, home free it seems.

We set off and I notice that this driver is a lot less clean looking. I obviously don't qualify for the best attention any more. Never mind.

No words are spoken as usual. Until I see a tractor starting to turn out in front of us. "Look out!" I scream. We are skidding to a halt and might just clip the tractor. I look over my shoulder and see the truck, too fast…

Carl's Story

I have been scanning the papers for a week now and no more from Portugal. Even Google has been quiet on news. I have been asking the question 'Manslaughter, Murder, Police' every day and nothing. The only hit was an accident close to East Midlands Airport. It seems that a car was hit by a tractor and then crushed, and I mean really totalled, by a truck that couldn't stop.

The tractor driver and the truck driver both disappeared before the police arrived and there were two bodies in the car. Very messy but no one was going to get out of a truck and tractor sandwich like that.

Well, that wife of mine is behaving strangely. One day down the next fine. I am just carrying on normally, making enough for her spending habits. She certainly goes through the money almost as fast as I make it, but I am stashing a bit aside. If she does not straighten up soon, I think we will have to go in different directions.

I just need to work out how best to get rid of her. Nothing drastic like that dude Jane may or may not have 'offed', so she never wants to come after me.

I have moved offices and am running under a name she does not know and she never really knew any details. I always shredded anything that had an address on it.

I could probably drop out of sight and she would never know.

I still have the old office and there is enough paperwork in there that would incriminate her if the police ever came after me. So maybe I should do that; disappear and leave enough evidence that she is involved. She has been creaming off a load of cash which would show if they looked, enough to make the waters really muddy for a while, then she would probably get off as there is no hard evidence.

So re-mortgage the house, siphon off the money and simply drop out. It's easy enough to get a new identity and all the bank accounts that go with it.

I might have to abandon trainers but there is enough designer gear out there. So yes, a new line of work in parallel with new names for a while, just in case. I will have to think about that.

Naomi's Story

It's been three weeks now since the 'murder' and I don't know where I am. I have good days when I can work and get stuff done, and then days where all I want to do is lay in bed. One day, I didn't get out of bed and I had not had a drink for a week but it felt like the worst hangover.

Like a black guilty cloud hanging over me.

I want to move back time and not do the things I did. I want that girl out of prison and I think I want to be rid of that philandering husband of mine. He has been so good and kind the last three weeks that I realise what life should have in it.

It's been nearly twenty years and I realise I have been in an abusive relationship all that time. Not that I have been harmed directly but emotionally. I have become hardened to his 'ways', accepting of his money in 'payment' for being the 'wife'.

He would have been better off with a housekeeper and an expensive tart, probably cheaper too!

Sitting here in the kitchen, I want to do something but unless I 'have' to, I can't. I wish I could go to the doctor but if I did, I might just spill the beans. What would happen then? Prison probably.

The Television News

"Police are investigating what could well turn out to be murder on the A42 near East Midlands Airport."

"At around 9.15 today, there was a traffic accident that appeared to be a car had hit a tractor and then the car was hit from behind by a following lorry."

"There are few details so far but it may be that the drivers of the tractor and lorry have disappeared."

"The road has been closed for four hours now and the crash site has already had a marquee erected over it. This does not normally happen in traffic incidents and leads us to suspect there is more to this story than meets the eye."

"Also breaking this afternoon, Teresa May said…"

Naomi's Story

Well, at least that distracted me a bit. Poor people, I wonder who was in the car and did the other drivers really just run away? It must have been their fault then.

Oh no, I must stop thinking this. I feel something that tells me it is murder like they are saying on the TV. Who was in the car and why if it was deliberate?

I realise that it is now 2.00 in the afternoon and I had better make a start on supper, at least look for something to cook. In desperation, I look into a fridge with some hard looking cheese and some salad that seems to be crawling away to die. NO! I must stop this thinking of death all the time!

In the freezer are some gourmet burgers and I know that the potatoes will clean up. OK so we can have nice chips. There is some coleslaw that is still in date and the tomatoes are mostly OK. That will do then, with a few herbs.

I get out all the ingredients and look at them, pathetic really. I know I must get a grip so I grab a couple of shopping bags and jump in the car. Tesco might not seem like it but at the moment, it is lifting my spirits to go there. A small bit of reality in my life as a potential murderer or at least someone who planned what could have been one.

The stark shop lights, concentrating on doing a weekly shop and what to really cook with the burgers distracts me and when I get home, I am feeling better. I open a nice white wine. I know it's only 4.00 now but I need cheering up. I would call a girlfriend but again I am afraid they would see inside me and see how bad I have been.

There is a knock on the window and I see my friend/neighbour, Annie, passing and getting to the back door. She comes in and says, "It's a bit early for the sauce, isn't it! Very bad, drinking alone and we can't have you on that slope, can we? Where are the glasses?"

She pours herself a large one and I steel myself and smile. "I was just back from Tesco. Pure hell trying to plan and cook for two when you never know when the old sod will turn up!"

"Tell me about it, darling. I know mine does come in at a set time. I can usually tell if the clocks fast when I hear the door go, but at least yours isn't so boring and always wanting the same food, meat spuds and veg. Sorry, I nearly forgot the gravy, heaven forbid!"

"I secretly put things like prunes in the gravy sometimes to try and give him the runs and then I sometimes make the gravy with too much flour so it sticks like shit to a blanket and tastes dry, but he never seems to notice as long as all the elements are on the plate."

We finish the wine and open another. I finish preparing the chips and the salad now looks like something 'proper', not tired and bedraggled like I was feeling.

"Shit, it's 6.00. I will have to go and get old 'borings' supper on. Looks like proper gravy granules tonight. Sorry to rush, bye."

I switch on the TV and the same story is now repeated, but there are extra pictures.

"It seems that the victims were both foreign. The police are reporting, one was an illegal immigrant of North African origin and the other seems to be a foreign national who was being driven to East Midlands Airport to catch a flight. The illegal immigrant appears to have been an un-registered private hire taxi driver."

"This leaves many questions unanswered. How did an illegal immigrant get to be driving an expensive car? Did the passenger think this was an official taxi and who exactly were these two people killed so tragically early today? This is Clive Midhurst of Sky news near East Midlands Airport."

The pictures are different in that. One is obviously a passport and the next is a photofit, meaning that the driver must have been badly smashed up for them to create that so soon.

Uncle Bob and One of His 'Sub Contractors'

"Any comeback yet?"

"No, they are still working back towards the hotel. They may or may not get there as the bill was removed and so were all the things we had time to get. We did get the briefcase which had all the paperwork and we put the replacement wallet and passport in his jacket."

"I used the spare passport with my photo as it matched the ticket so no one would be suspicious about missed flights. So what next?"

"Good; take the briefcase to the office and get yourself out of the country for a month."

"Thanks, boss. Anywhere I should go?"

"Just avoid home for the moment. Somewhere quiet in Spain, Portugal or Italy so you are with tourists would be good, so you don't stick out. Oh and drive, don't want any airport staff picking you up. Take a decent car but not too young."

"Will be done, briefcase by 11.00, over the border by noon?"

"Fine."

***

"Any loose ends to tidy up?"

"We have covered the car, cash paid and false addresses for the last two owners; the passport is a forgery, the illegal is untraceable and no family. That poor, stupid boy should have kept his pants on and then he would be alive."

"The hotel has CCTV but its poor quality, and it's almost certain that a staff member showed the husband the blonde going into his room and then identified him personally. I have seen the CCTV and its very grainy. The police will probably make the connection in which case, the husband will be in the frame for five minutes, till they realise he is a tosser who can't keep his wife happy."

Detective Inspector Will Knowles and Detective Sergeant Fred Wills Midlands Police

"So let me get this straight. We have two corpses, three vehicles, two stolen, plus one right off that seems to have nothing to trace it at all. Really nothing?"

"Yes, Sir. The tractor was nicked from a farm nearby and the truck was from miles away, but in both cases, the drivers were anesthetised so they would not be able to report them missing. The car has changed hands twice and although, the transactions are registered to proper addresses, one looks like it was where the driver was living and the other is a short term holiday let, lots of random post that never gets delivered."

"The insurance was from a different broker both times and paid in cash, and the tax was bought at post offices again in cash. Not illegal but suspicious as its all dead ends. The driver details from the insurance show the same picture which looks like the illegal both times so we suspect that the licences were obtained fraudulently."

"The passport on the passenger was forged, but very good and he had no credit cards, which is strange. He had a reasonable amount of euros and some pounds, but no ticket to fly anywhere. I checked with the airlines and there were three no shows for lunchtime flights. We are tracking them down now, hopefully one of them will be our man."

"This looks very well organised. The drugging of the two drivers of the stolen vehicles shows it was most probably a hit. Two rival drug gangs maybe?"

"That seems likely but they don't fit the profile of ethnicity of all the ones we know are operating and the precision of the faked crash shows that they knew where the car would be, they must have been following it. Is there any CCTV showing traffic before the accident and did anyone around at the time see anyone who has not come forward?"

"Wow, boss, that is going to take some time asking all the drivers who they did and didn't see! The nearest camera is outside a petrol station about two miles away. It's set up to capture any drive aways but I should be able to get something. I'll need two extra bodies to do the CCTV and the checking. Can you arrange that?"

"Yes, it's not a problem. The chief constable has authorised whatever we need. We need to rule out terrorists as quickly as possible and the media are going mad for detail and we don't have anything. We will look pretty stupid if we can't trace something. What about the two vehicles?"

"Sorry, boss, the tractor was ploughing a field and it seems from the tobacco we found scattered that the tractor driver was caught having a quick fag. The truck was on its way to a quarry and would then have had a two hour drive to deliver the aggregate, so going missing for three hours would not have raised any suspicion. Best guess is that when he stopped for early breakfast, he got back in the cab and was mugged."

"He was found in a remote public toilet, in the ladies, bound and gagged and the door had an out of order sticker on it. Only when he woke up and heard someone come in did he start kicking the door, but that was nearly noon; been sitting there with no trousers and a pair of girls trainers showing under the door."

"Trainers give us a clue?"

"No. Primani, I am afraid."

"Primani?"

"Sorry, boss, Primark. Thought everyone knew that?"

"OK you're forgiven. This is looking very, very professional. Get digging and get me some answers."

"Yes, boss. I'll try."

***

"Anything, Sergeant?"

"Well, boss, we have run down of the no shows at the airport and all have a good reason to not catch their planes. In other words, none of them is our man. Maybe he wasn't going to the airport but with all that luggage, he must have been going somewhere."

"Also a lot of his clothes have had the labels removed. We can trace them but no way to tell when and where they were bought; only very skimpy information like when the ranges were being sold. Looks like they were purchased over a five to ten year period."

"Wait, you can only guess five years or ten? Come on, better than that please."

"Sorry, boss, really most of this stuff is expensive and tending towards the classic stuff that is sold year after year, so although all the gear has probably been purchased in the UK, we don't know how long over. The newer stuff we have traced and we have some CCTV of a clean cut guy, could be north eastern European, Polish possibly."

"We have interviewed the sales assistants who sold the stuff and he seems to have spoken English almost like a native, saying he was either born here or came early or had English influence early on, or he was being clever. The iPad was never registered, only switched on, but we did get a break there. The Wi-Fi code indicates a hotel and we are going there later today to see if we can get anywhere."

"Why so long to get that last bit?"

"The iPad passcodes are not easy. It took the best guy in London a week to break it. No cloud account set up and it was only used to browse the web for clothes and tech stuff like the new stuff we found. All of that was bought for cash in the local town as was the iPad."

"No clues at all."

"No, boss. No porn, no email, nothing that takes us anywhere but back up our own backsides. My feeling is that this is very bad. It's almost like he was a spy and we can't even trace where he lived, given that he must have stayed somewhere in the UK to get the clothes."

"Have we given him to the spooks?"

"Yes, you did authorise that remember, and they have come back with nothing at all. Even when they are hiding someone, we can get a hint but this guy just didn't exist!"

"OK any DNA matches at all?"

"Nothing at all yet. It takes a time as we are sending it round the world now because of the terrorist thing."

Carl's Story

This is getting rather spooky. I am really worried now.

I bang on Dave's door. He should have been back to me but has not and because of all the other stuff I had forgotten I wanted more info.

"Dave, where have you been? It's been days and I was expecting some more information."

"Carl, (a wheeze) come in (more wheezing)."

Dave is limping and has the stain of a black eye.

"Sorry, mate, I got mugged while I was waiting to ask around." He was obviously in pain and could only speak half properly while sitting down.

"Is this anything to do with you asking questions?"

I wait while he takes in a few painful breaths.

"Possibly but it seems too random. I went outside for a fag and a guy was just lighting up and offered me a light." More wheezing. "He wandered off and as I took the second drag, I get a kidney punch that hurts so much I go down. Next I am getting a kicking and my wallet, phone and car keys go."

"They stole your car?"

"No, just the keys, probably wanted to turn this place over, but I don't have the address in my wallet luckily. If they had taken the letter from my other pocket, we would probably be sitting on the floor!"

"So what happened after they hit you?"

"It was a light beating, thank god. I have one broken rib, so nothing new there." A laugh and then a pained cough. "I ended in hospital at nearly midnight after a good Samaritan spotted me in the bushes, almost like I was a bit drugged. Then I had to explain to the police, then they found a locksmith. Hey, the cops know some wicked people, better than anyone I know. The guy just walked up to the door, fiddled with the lock and we were in!"

"The cops were with me to make sure I was who I say, passport etcetera, but once I could prove that, they gave me a lift back to my car. I had a set of spare keys for the flat and the car here luckily, I managed to get back here."

"Then the painkillers wore off and I have been struggling for the last few days, just drinking water and eating dry biscuits 'cause that's all that was here. Carl, mate, can you get me some pies or something. I am starving, and some milk. I would kill for a tea or a coffee."

So I pop down the corner shop and get the poor old sod some painkillers, a pint of milk, some dried sandwiches and a pie that is only one day out of date and take it back. After the tea, he starts to look a bit better. Even starts moving less painfully.

"Sorry, mate, I failed so I guess you don't even have to pay me." But I take pity on him and drop him a couple and I am left with a real question to answer.

I sit in the car and wonder if this was because he asked the questions. Dave's phone would provide a direct line to my house and so to me. If this Tony guy was into something dodgy, then who knows. Probably best to let it drop, but first I am going to go to the area and just suss it out.

I actually have a great idea. I arrange to meet someone I do business with for a lunch. That will not raise any suspicions, get a bit of business done and see where this 'Tony' lived and presumably drank.

Well, that was an eye opener! Police signs all over the place 'have you seen this man?' So it is 'Tony' and he is a good looking guy and it allows me to ask the barman what it is all about.

Seemingly since Dave's visit, these have all appeared as Tony is the 'missing' guy from Portugal, so that closes the circle and means that Dave was just unlucky. I do get a lot of volunteered information. Barmen are always either quiet or like this one full of bullshit wanting to look big.

No one has a clue where he worked or what he did. Seems to have had a string of nice cars so the car dealer thing would fit. Strange that no one local had ever bought anything from him; very strange but I don't think I want to dig any more.

Mark the Vape and Uncle Bob

"Any repercussions on the guy who was asking questions?"

"Yea a bit. That guy Carl was asking about trying to pretend otherwise, but the bar he was in was the one where the other guy had been asking. Our local help happened to be in there having a beer. I have bunged him £50 for being awake and to keep him quiet. Told him there was a link that we didn't want anyone to know about."

Detective Inspector Will Knowles and Detective Sergeant Fred Wills

"So we have a missing person who fits the frame for the guy from Portugal and he disappeared at the right time?"

"Yes, boss, always kept a low profile, never any trouble, never got drunk, was seen with a string of attractive women but only ever getting out of the car and going into the flat. We have sent the DNA to the Portuguese and they say it is a match."

"Who would think that a nice looking girl like that could have done for him! He must have a bad side to have upset her. Do you recon she found the Rohypnol and turned the tables on him?"

"Does not sound right. He has a string of nice looking girls who don't seem to need any coercion so why pick up someone, apparently at the airport, wine her and dine her and then she kills him. She claims complete innocence. If she had been attacked, then she would say so but she is sticking to the story that he disappeared."

"Were the women tarts?"

"Could have been but it's still not a pattern."

"Anything from the posters? What about the people you primed with info?"

"Nothing. They have only said people ask about the poster and they give them the info and that is it!"

"Dead end then more or less."

"Yes, boss, no one to chase up, sorry."

Uncle Bob and Mark the Vape

"Where are they?"

"Nowhere, useless lot. You would have thought that the DNA would have linked up by now. We know it will and then the shit will hit the fan for a while, then everyone will say 'why' then it will be back into the room with no doors."

"Sure we are that tight?"

"Yes, the cops have not even realised that Tony was at the hotel. I suppose the passport picture that has been all over the media being the wrong one is slowing them down."

Detective Inspector Will Knowles and Detective Sergeant Fred Wills

"Autopsy back yet?"

"Yes, boss, and there is something odd. The passport picture is apparently wrong. They did a reconstruction from the skull and it looks nothing like the passport. He would have got out OK but when you make a 3D model, you can see all sorts of differences, but with glasses and five o'clock shadow, it looks fine."

"So we knew the passport was false but we had believed the picture was genuine. That makes a big difference. Get the photo fit on the news tonight. This is why we have not found out where he was staying or anything about him. God, I must be slipping; you didn't hear that last bit OK?"

"OK, boss, and I don't think anyone could have picked that up. There was pretty little left of the skull after thirty tons of truck had ironed it!"

***

"Boss, I've got two calls. One from the Belvedere hotel and one from the mob who are the liaison with the Portuguese on the murder, both say they know our man."

"Well, sort of bingo then. Get all the info and make sure you get the DNA checked. Why didn't it cross reference before?"

"Well, the DNA that was sent to Portugal would not be on the national database as he was not a criminal. It would have shown up in a week or so but not until it went through the registration. All they were doing was checking that they had found the correct flat for him and that he had never been in the girls before, all self-enclosed. Only when they failed to get a proper background on him, would it have showed up."

"Wait a minute, did you say they still don't know who he is?"

"Yes, boss, this is an enigma inside an enigma now. We have someone we can't trace and when we 'find' him, it turns out that he does not have a proper past at all; someone who was a mystery before we got him."

"When will we get a definite on the DNA?"

"A couple of days, why?"

"Well, the poor girl who is being held for his murder obviously didn't do it, so we had better warn everyone to be ready to eat humble pie. We might come out of this well yet, because we at least unravelled what happened."

"Good thought, boss. Do you want to do that or perhaps you should suggest the super does it? 'Sorry to bring the news' sort of. He will enjoy rubbing the others noses in it and we won't be considered the baddies. No point in upsetting our 'friends' from down there."

"Very good point. Get me the file and I will take it upstairs now. Quiet words in ears, etcetera, very good."

Jane's Story

I don't know what is happening. I have been moved to a much nicer cell, well not a cell even more like a hotel suite. Still no inside door handles, but a living room with a little kitchenette, a bathroom and a bedroom. No one will tell me what is going on and my solicitor is not here until five.

"It seems that the police now believes you may have been some sort of innocent bystander, not innocent yet but maybe not guilty of such bad things. So they want to soften you up before you get out and don't think of suing them for wrongful arrest. You would not get anywhere in any case as they have behaved correctly in the circumstances."

My mind spins. I know I am innocent but what has changed their minds? Have they found Tony alive? Still no one will tell me anything, but at least I feel clean now. Somehow, although innocent, I felt dirty because everyone thought I was.

My solicitor returns.

"I can't get any real information at the moment but if you agree, you are to be sent to England for interview in another crime. They won't tell me what but it is connected and very closely."

***

"So, miss, come this way. We will have to handcuff you because you are under arrest but we can try and make it not too obvious. Please use the toilet now as it will be difficult on the plane."

On the plane, a scarf is draped over the chain and the woman police officer is pleasant but not talkative so I feel more relaxed. At least, in the UK I will be able to understand everyone.

"Now, miss, remember you are under arrest in Portugal and have come here voluntarily. At this time, we cannot answer any questions, though I can see you have many you want to ask. So please be patient and answer all the questions we have truthfully as it may harm your defence of any crime if you lie to us. You will be given a transcript of what you say and will be required to sign that. Do you understand?"

I nod quietly. I am so nervous again. Am I supposedly guilty of something else? I request that information.

"Your solicitor will be here directly to guide you through the process. He has been briefed with as much information as we can release and you will have an hour before we get started."

My solicitor is very young, as young as the last one was greasy, but he seems confident that I am not going to be tried for murder or even manslaughter but then adds, "As long as you are not really involved, they had you bang to rights before and I suppose that could be true now too."

"Is the brief with her?"

"Yes, twenty minutes now. So what is going on?"

"Well, it seems that the guy we thought died in Portugal actually bought it on the A42 ten days ago but it's still not at all clear what has been going on. According to this woman's story, she met the victim at Gatwick a month ago, he disappeared under strange circumstances and looked like he had died over there, only to die here ten days later."

"So he died twice, once pretend and once real. There must be some big crime going on behind this. Are we being very careful?"

"Yes, boss. We have not let the press know that she is back here and the Portuguese have lost interest because it didn't happen on their patch. She is still technically under arrest there but until we find out what happened, we are being very cagey."

"So she could be somehow in on both bits?"

"Not sure, boss, it still does not make sense. She seems to have been framed and if he had not died then, she would have probably gone down over there. If she is involved, then she is deep in it, knowing that she will get off when the body turns up alive after the supposed killing. She could be making the perfect alibi and sending a very serious message to others, but we don't know what the underlying crime is yet."

"So from a right mess where two cases come together we now have a bigger and stickier mess?"

"Yes, boss. We only have this woman and now a guy in the midlands who may have had a motive to kill the guy."

"Who is that?"

"Seems he is the husband of a woman who the deceased had at least a night with. The wife was stupid in the extreme as they only had one car and she used the Sat Nav to get to the hotel where the bloke was staying. She didn't clear the destination so he wondered where she had been, she said out with a female friend in town."

"He asked the friend's husband saying something had gone missing on a particular night and he thought that his wife might have dropped in. Answer was no so he got really suspicious and went to the hotel with a picture of the wife, paid someone a few quid and got to see his missus going into a hotel room with another man. Earlier on, on the morning of the murder, the bloke punched the deceased and knocked him to the ground, but no report or complaint."

"How come the autopsy didn't pick the injury up?"

"Boss, you saw the remains, and it was only an hour before so the bruising had not really started, it looked like one big trauma."

"Could the husband have done it?"

"No way, boss, he is, shall we say, a little challenged. His wife says she only stays because he keeps a steady job. Usual not rocking the boat, he must normally turn a blind eye to her having a bit of a fling, but somehow this time he boiled over!"

"Sure?"

"More sure about that than anything else in this case, and he had an alibi as he was at work on time as usual that day. So he went to the hotel, seemingly for three days before as well, got the guy's routine and on the day he checked out, he decked him and walked off."

"OK don't chase any shadows there, we have enough everywhere else!"

Uncle Bob and Mark the Vape

"How are they doing?"

"Better; the DNA has hit at last. I have been wondering, should we put that guy Carl in the frame so the circle is closed? Quite funny that his wife paid us. I guess we are not giving refunds?"

"No, she can't find us. That PI only has an email, you had better close that. No, don't, that would be perfect if Carl were the one setting it up and paying for the hit, work out some details and come back to me. That way we still exist; it looks like he is taking revenge for losing his girlfriend. Are all the eBay links closed down?"

"Yes, we always do that every time, I will work out how to implicate him and get back to you to give the go ahead."

"Talk to me tomorrow with the details."

Jane's Story—With Detective Inspector Donald Jones in London

"Well, miss, your story now checks out but we still have a dead man on our hands, but as you were in Portugal, you could not have done it. We do, however, need to hold you still until the Portuguese authorities ask us to. However, you will be re-arrested as we need to rule you out of the actual murder."

So you only met Mr Peterson at Gatwick, so we need to establish a few facts. First, why did he disappear and second, why did he die later. You could still be involved as you were the last person we know to have seen him when he seemingly died, and because of that, you are still a very strong suspect. Conspiracy if not the actual act of murder.

"Now we will start with your movements in the month before your trip. We have your electronic diary from your phone and laptop and see your pattern of behaviour. Would you like to take us through that month and we will make a few notes to go back over?"

***

"OK, we have been through your version of what you did and we can confirm that what you have told us is correct. Only your Tuesday and Thursday afternoons need to be clarified. Where did you go and who did you see?"

***

"So you met this guy from the gym for sex every Tuesday and Thursday. Who is he?"

"Yes, there is a Carl at your gym and as you said he is married. We will be discreet but we will need to interview him and possibly his wife; we only have your word as to your connection with him. Now did he ever come to your flat. No, I see. So we won't find any DNA associations then. That's a pity; it does make life easier if we can verify things."

Carl's Story

Bloody cops been here and interviewed me. I suppose that I should be grateful that they didn't pick me up at home, that was decent of them. I hope they don't analyse the computers too carefully. I don't really break laws but its close. Still they said I can have them back tomorrow as they just want a copy at the moment.

Fancy arriving with a search warrant and confiscation of computer order. They are not looking at the business thank heavens, because all the company information is there and plain to see.

Detective Inspector Will Knowles and Detective Sergeant Fred Wills

"What did we find on his computer then?"

"Well, boss, it's not good. he seemed Mr cool but there are transactions on an eBay account in his wife's name and it seems 'she' bought a load of cars all the same price over a very short period, looks like money laundering. Either he is very cool or doesn't realise we can get this detail off his hard drive. We have not arrested him but have a loose watch on him, in case his movement patterns change. No difference so far."

"Anything else?"

"Yes, there are small parts of files that reference the same drug used on the two mugged guys and Rohypnol. So definite traces over a month ago. Also he has been accessing his wife's bank account on his computer. We need to look at the computers at his house."

"OK, you had better get a warrant for the search and his arrest if we have real traces."

"OK, boss, will do. Heavy boots?"

"No, low key. Tell the wife some financial irregularities. From what you tell me about him, that will not surprise her."

***

"What's on her computer then?"

"Nothing, boss. No eBay, no internet access to that bank account, though she does have a debit card that is on it and she draws money out regularly."

"What is her story?"

"Very close, wanted a solicitor; it's the same one Carl is using now and it's 'no comment'."

"How about his story? Does he break any laws? He seems to make a lot for one guy on his own."

"He does get close, but the only thing he does that is suspect is bribe a couple of people in the shipping company to change the destination of containers. Nothing illegal as far as I can see, probably breaks some trade regulations, but then its close. I must ask why the same trainers cost twice as much here as they do in Africa! Bloody rip off it seems to me."

"So we have him and all we need is one more bit of evidence and we can charge him with murder?"

"Conspiracy, boss. Nothing to tie him to any actions and cast iron alibi for 9.15 on the day of the murders. He could be a money man and facilitator."

Carl and Detective Inspector Will Knowles

"So, Sir, we have your computer and temporary files dated a month ago, showing your interest in certain drugs that link you with some very unsavoury matters. Would you care to elaborate?"

"No comment."

"Right, Sir, then we will have to pull your home and office to pieces. It's going to be a full forensic sweep as we need to establish DNA of all the people who have visited you, so I need a list please and contact details."

Uncle Bob and His IT Sub Contractor

"What did you plant?"

"The passport in a bin outside in an envelope he had licked. Will have Tony's DNA and fingerprints, handled it with gloves so it looks like he dumped it carelessly."

Carl and Detective Inspector Will Knowles

"Well, Sir, we now have one piece of evidence that you can't question."

"I have never seen that passport before!"

"Well, Sir, it's from the waste bin outside your office and you licked the envelope. You have been careless. I suggest that you and your solicitor here take a bit of time to discuss this and you come up with something a bit more convincing."

Carl and His Solicitor

"I don't understand, I am being framed here. Who planted that passport? It can't be the police as it links me to the murder. Help me please, what is going on?"

"Carl, I have no idea. I don't think they are doing anything dodgy, so it must be the lot who did for the guy who was supposed to have been in Portugal."

Detective Inspector Will Knowles and Detective Sergeant Fred Wills

"Can we charge him?"

"I suggest we wait until we get a few more details. He should by rights be ready to sing very soon, making our work much simpler."

"I want that envelope gone over with a fine tooth comb. I want any specs of dust examined and I want to know if it could have been contaminated in any way. His DNA on the glue strip is all we have and its addressed to someone, but never posted. We have to ask why, it's a weak link. No finger prints even on the passport or where he would have had to hold it to lick, which is a worry."

Uncle Bob and His IT Sub Contractor

"What did you do then?"

"When his missus was out, I went in and cleaned her computer and tablet. I kept the files and put them onto his computer, so that was eBay and the bank. Plus, I put a trace of that email account we set up and deleted on there. They can see it but I doubt that Hotmail will keep deleted account details for long. We will have to find out. It's only going to bury him deeper."

"DNA?"

"Here I am hoping what I have done works. I was suitably gowned and gloved up, so none of my DNA could get on the envelope. I looked like someone out of that hospital programme!"

"He was a gum chewer so I moistened some chewing gum with warm distilled water and then rolled the residue on the envelope flap. I did it with several pieces so it should stick. I have never had to do it before so fingers crossed."

Uncle Bob and Mark the Vape

"Where are they with him now?"

"He is in custody on suspicion of murder or manslaughter; his wife is free but they now have a car outside in case she wants to skip. I think she might be a bit of a weak link, but one we can capitalise on. She must realise that we are doing this and if she loves that guy, she will come clean and clear him, or they will both be charged with conspiring."

"Your IT guy did a good job and she is in the clear, no links with anything to do with us. Those links are on his computer so it looks like he is involved somehow. As he was not, they will only have it as circumstantial evidence and can't build a case round it. Same goes for the DNA as there are no fingerprints then."

Naomi's Story

Well, that is a turn up for the books. It must be the people I paid to frame that girl and somehow the plan went wrong, and the guy who was supposed to pretend to die has been killed, but that is going to mean the girl gets away with it. I don't really care. I will stop having nightmares when she is released. I am worried about Carl. They have framed him for the murder.

I can't tell anyone in case they come after me. I know they will kill me and I don't want to die, even though I do deserve to be where Carl is. On the bright side, I will be rid of him forever and as long as I can get my hands on his money, I will be fine. This house is paid for and my account will be unfrozen soon they tell me when there is proof that the money is not from the proceeds of crime.

They must be very clever because the eBay cars were bought through my tablet computer and the police found no trace on mine but did on Carl's, so they must have somehow moved them. I do like the way the police are treating me as a bit of a victim. I know they still think I might be in cahoots with Carl, but the thick innocent wife who knows nothing seems to be working.

I am wondering what I should do? Contact the private eye perhaps as he made the contacts.

Private Eye Steve Morris

Life does throw up some odd stuff. I have just had a garbled conversation with that bloke's wife. Apparently, he is in jail and suspected of being involved with the murder of the guy who was supposed to have died in Portugal. I could not make sense of what she was saying. I will have to do some digging.

There might be a few more quid to be milked from this. I might get that week away yet!

Detective Inspector Will Knowles and Detective Sergeant Fred Wills

"Can we charge her with anything?"

"No, Sir, afraid not. It seems that when he went out in the morning, she never knew when he would be back, and that is backed up by her friends and neighbours. A couple even said they think Carl is a bit bent, can't see how he made all the money they had stashed. Can we keep the money as proceeds of crime?"

"No, Sir, the accounts for the company seem to be in order. He even paid all his corporation tax and personal tax. He did have the wife on the payroll which is wrong as she didn't do any work, but it's hardly going to worry the revenue as she was paying tax even though she didn't know."

"So we unfreeze the accounts?"

"I see no reason not to. I don't know if the wife will want to carry the business on, but perhaps we should ask her and also let her write a letter to Carl and see if he wants her to, no verbal communication, but it might throw up a lead or two if she will. Especially as there are now two containers of trainers waiting to be sold in his warehouse."

"OK get one of the business boys to run their eyes over the books again and suggest that they go and see her as a gesture of goodwill, should get her well off guard and might get us a new lead. Is she a director and shareholder?"

"Yes, she is, Sir, so perfectly entitled to take over. She will need to get control of the bank accounts but her solicitor will help her with that I am sure."

Carl's Story

Well, I don't know who I upset but they have screwed me completely. They have two good bits of evidence, one DNA, how they got that onto the envelope I don't know. I know how they got the files onto my computer, that would not be difficult for a good techie but what was Naomi doing sending all that money via eBay on cars that didn't exist?

I am beginning to know how Jane must have felt. I didn't do this but I am in the frame. They can't do me for murder; the closest will be conspiracy or aiding and abetting, but that is going to be five to ten as I can't grass anyone as I don't know. My brief is useless as he thinks I am guilty and I can't talk to Naomi.

Well, it's taken two hours but I have worked out what that daft cow was doing, not happy about it but I can't blame her really. She must have been planning to leave and that was her way of hiding the money. Somewhere there will be a bank account in a false name with the money in it.

The cops are not bothered in trying to trace it as they can't get any further than one step after the transaction. One PayPal account that has been closed is as far as they have bothered to go.

The letter that she sent me was obviously written by someone else, probably the solicitor and I have to decide what to do. Should I trust her with the business? I guess I have nothing to lose as the worst she can do is wind it up. It never owes any money so it's not going to be liquidated by a creditor.

I had better draft a formal reply telling her to and telling the bank to accept her. I want to see her and warn her that I am going to be away for a while. I can't see what else I can do. With luck, she will still be around and so will some of the money when I get out.

Maybe once this has happened, they will let her see me.

Carl and Naomi

"Naomi, love, I worked out what you were doing on eBay, but please don't leave me now. I need you to look after the money and if you want, the business until I get out. If you want to leave me, then can we just split it all 50/50 and call it a day. We were not that bad together, were we?"

"Carl, it's OK. I will do as you ask. While you are away, I will keep things going and when you come out, it will all be split up. You will have to trust me. You have no choice now and it's rather nice being in control of you for a change. I do care for you so be careful. I will come and visit you."

Naomi and Detective Inspector Will Knowles

"How long will he get, officer?"

"Five years I think. All we have on him is the passport and that links him to a murder and makes him guilty of conspiracy. Did you never have any suspicions about what he was up to?"

"No, he worked, I spent and kept house, we had sex but it turned into a bit of a sham I suppose."

"So you never knew the girl who was arrested in Portugal?"

"His tart you mean, yes I read the papers. He is 'linked to her' it says, meaning they were probably at it. Did you say she went to the same gym? I may have even seen her. I did work for their brochure a couple of months ago."

***

Thank god that private detective never came forward. He could have completely screwed me up, so all's well that ends well. Carl will be away, I will get to have a bit of fun with his money and tinker with the business. It looks like a piece of cake to run. I suppose he was not that clever really, just street wise.

Detective Inspector Will Knowles and Detective Sergeant Fred Wills

"So do we have anything that we can really use as evidence? It's all very tenuous, we could really do with a 'hand in the till'."

"We have the DNA and fingerprints, but no way of proving that the guy actually had the passport as its clean otherwise, so we have a passport that 'may' have been used by the deceased. We are stuck; there will be no prosecution unless we can link it closer."

"Well, boss, if we can't actually charge him, then why not release him and watch him?"

"That will cost a fortune. Yes, I know it would work but we don't have the budget."

"OK so let's refreeze the bank accounts, let the bills get paid and let him go. Wait a moment. No, don't freeze the accounts, but put a warning so that if he tries to move more than a grand we know about it, and get the details of the credit cards and they can do the following for us."

"Do we let him go on bail or free and clear?"

"Free and clear but with a warning about not leaving the country; we will seize his passport too. Also written letter saying he may be rearrested as the enquiry is on-going."

Carl's Story

Result—something must have come up, they are letting me go. They said it was only a technicality but they have to release me. I don't even have to report every twenty-four hours so I can get on with stuff and try and find out who it is that is trying to frame me.

First stop, home, to get clean and see the wife. If I am not going away, then I don't need to brief her how to manage things either.

Actually, I will give her all the access though, she needs to see how things work in case I am banged up again.

Carl and Naomi

"Carl, you're home, thank goodness, I was worried about you. What is happening? Why did they let you go? Are you really free? Did you learn anything from them? I tried to get them to tell me what was going on but they blanked me. I thought they were going to arrest me and it was only when the solicitor started to make threats, they backed off."

"Wow, slow down, girl. No, they didn't tell me anything, just being released on a technicality at the moment, but that will probably mean I am in the clear."

"So, love, I did learn a few things; squirrelling away money it seems was one of them. Why did you need to? I thought I looked after you well enough. I know I am not perfect, well even very good in some ways, but we need to get through this and I think we need each other, so can we agree to help each other at least until all this mess is over."

"Carl, of course, I want to help. It might be good for me to learn how your business works. That was one of the things that in the past has probably contributed to why I didn't trust you as much. By the way, that was why I was squirrelling away a few pounds in case I was left the way it looked like I was going to be."

"OK, love, let's have a quiet night in and in the morning, we will go to the office and I will start your training course. I need a glass or three of wine, some of your lovely cooking and a good night's sleep."

Naomi's Story

Well, that went better than I expected. The old fellow was shattered. Well, he certainly enjoyed most of a bottle of that decent red we keep in and the steaks I got out of the freezer were perfect even if I say so myself.

And then after he 'perked up' and we had a lovely time before we went to sleep. He is good at it, that is something I would have missed. I suspect that even if we did get divorced, there might be the odd bit of 'friends with benefits'. I am looking forward to learning.

I might be the boring housewife but I could do with the mental stimulation, and a bit of a challenge will do me no harm. If I find him with that woman again though, I will be pretty mad and he will get marching orders.

Carl's Story

Well, that was a good day. My wife is brighter than I gave her credit for. Also she has tidied up the office, got the filing up to date, catalogued all the processes that I use so she can replicate them. I think another half-day and she could take over without too many problems. I have let my contacts know that my new assistant might be in contact instead of me, so if I am 'away' for any reason, I will be happy she can manage the business.

Off to buy her a work phone now and she is making supper at home again, might get lucky again!

"Hi, I need a decent phone and a new contract. Look me up, this is my number."

"Yes, Sir. The best deal is to add the new contract on to your account and the most popular phone at the moment is this one easy to use. The same operating system as yours and her private one, just the updated version of the phone she has already."

"OK that will do fine. By the way, do you have any really cheap pay as you go phones, just a simple one, sim only agreement."

"Yes, Sir, this one is very reasonable. Will you want to add it to the contract as well?"

"No, I will pay for it separately. Did you say £50? I will pay you cash for that one; it's for a friend."

"Keep the receipt then, Sir, in case there are any warranty problems."

Well, that is good. I have bought a phone to act as a 'burner' as I want to see if Jane is OK and try and find out what is happening from her perspective. I suspect that Naomi will be trawling the phone records, looking for strange numbers that have not been called since Jane's arrest in Portugal. Naomi is clever enough to do that.

Get this set up and transfer the number over and I can reconnect if she wants to talk. I don't think I want to get involved again, that would be too dangerous, but I cannot forget how good we were in bed.

Crikey, that was quick! Jane replied within a minute and she does want to meet. We chatted after the text. I said to call if she wanted to talk but would understand if not and she came straight back. Good to hear her voice and she seems to be in the clear.

Jane's Story

"Well, miss, we can confirm there will be no charges against you. Although, your boyfriend has not confessed, we are fairly sure he arranged to have your new lover killed. We can't fathom why the strange goings on in Portugal but what we do know as fact may be sufficient to put him away for a while."

"We may release him for a while until we have managed to gather all the evidence, we need but I don't think you have to worry about him. He will have an exclusion order on him so he should not contact you."

So I am free. Two months I have lived a nightmare; the television has painted me as on the side of the devil, but that is better than being in jail. I don't believe that about Carl though. He was never possessive at all. We even took a 'break' for a month once when he had a trip to go on and I was off as well, just a 'no strings' thing.

We actually met back at the gym by accident and the spark was still there so we started again; he could be so cheeky.

Certainly, no angel but that was part of the attraction.

Now that is strange. I am thinking about him and he sends me a text from a new phone. We will probably meet up soon but I will have to keep it under cover as he is not supposed to contact me.

I guess it's back to work. I have heard from one company that don't want to use me anymore but I know that most of my clients will still use me. I wonder what really happened. I will never know now and there is too much darkness in it all for me to start digging. I might have to emigrate, Australia maybe, so I am as far away as possible from this mess.

The police take me home. On the way, my newly returned phone rings, one of my oldest clients.

"Jane, where have you been? We have been trying to get hold of you for a month. There is an assignment for you but the meeting is today at 3 pm, can you make it?"

"Mike, does it have to be today? I am a bit busy…"

"Sorry but yes, the manufacturer's representative is leaving this evening for New York then Tokyo. If you want the assignment, then it's today or he will get someone else. We would rather have you on board as we can liaise with you more easily."

I sigh, I can change clothes and just make it. "OK, Mike, I will see you at 3.00."

The policeman escorts me up to the flat. I let myself in and see that it's a bit dusty, but nothing serious has happened. "Thank you, officer, I can manage now."

"OK, miss, take care and when we know anything, we will call. If you have not heard in two weeks, then call us. We may be able to release your passport."

A very quick shower, a trip to the cashpoint and a cab gets me to the meeting with moments to spare. The flat looked a lot more homely with my clothes strewn around.

Well, the meeting works out fine. I have the assignment which will take my mind off things. Luckily, it seems my new notoriety has not spread as far as I had thought it might. Also, I suspect that my clients don't really give a stuff as long as I apply my brain to their problem.

I head off to a bar where some friends hang out and after a few drinks and a lot of explaining, I eat a quiet meal alone. After a couple of hours of quiet reflection, I am ready. I didn't want to just go home. If I am restarting my life, I want it to be better. This ordeal has hurt me badly but I can't let it show or be bitter about it. Perhaps, I will see a counsellor and let it out that way; the police did say they could put me in touch with someone.

When I get back, the same constable as before is waiting for me outside…

Naomi's Story

He came back! The police let him out, even he can't tell why. I now have access to everything. I know how much money he has; that was an eye opener!

He said it was in case they rearrested him. I even have his contacts in the shipping company so I know who to get the containers redirected. So he must trust me and I assume wants to stay with me. Funny how being on the brink of splitting up seems to have brought us closer.

We had one whole day in the office and I have learned everything I need to know. My 'training' will carry on over the next few days. He needs a day catching up with people, but I now know who they are and what their roles are. I can access the phone contracts so I can keep an eye.

I have worked out the girls number from the historic calls, always the day before they met up, and I know the dates because I have access to the credit card statements. It did cause a bit of pain but I am pretty much over that; still an open sore but it is healing.

It was a little strange but still somehow comforting how he got up early, grabbed a cup of coffee and went off as usual. He even left me with the job of going into the bank with the letters of authorisation. He had phoned them and had the proper paperwork sent over by courier. The neighbour was trying to read all the paperwork upside down, which was funny, when she was witnessing everything.

I was still amazed when the bank manager welcomed me personally and ushered me into his office to do all the paperwork. I guess money talks and somewhere in the region of five million talks a lot!

No wonder he didn't miss that four hundred thousand I squirrelled away until I spent half of it on buying the 'cars'.

Jane, a Constable and Detective Inspector Will Knowles

The uniformed policeman was very friendly but in a slightly odd way, almost like he was pretending.

"Hello again, there is one thing I have been asked to check with you. Can we go up to your flat please?"

We walk up and I get a strange feeling that something is wrong. It's the way the policeman who was friendly before now has a different demeanour, slightly stiff.

I unlock the door and walk in.

There are blood spatters on one of the walls and the furniture is all over the place. I faint.

Detective Inspector Will Knowles and Detective Sergeant Fred Wills

"How is she?"

"She seems fine, a little weak, but that's not a surprise. What happened?"

"She went to the meeting, then had drinks with some friends, then there are two hours where she says she was in a restaurant, but we can't be certain of that as the waitress had gone off and is not on until tomorrow."

"So there are two hours where she could have come back?"

"Yes, and we have CCTV showing someone dressed like her entering the building with a stocky man, who is the dead ringer for that Carl."

"Then the same woman comes out again an hour later. Then ten minutes after that, a removals company bring out a small wardrobe which looks to be much heavier than it should be. We get the call about noise between the two events. Someone was 'moving furniture badly or fighting' according to the report."

"Any CCTV on the van?"

"Yes, you won't like this, plain white transit, number plate clearly visible"

"What's bad about that?"

"The number plate is false. It's registered to Cardiff police and was in their car park when this happened."

"That is very cheeky. So they are not going to worry as long as we don't see their faces."

"Yes, Sir, and the local station had a car round just after the van left, but they were not really expecting anyone to be hurt; just a small domestic at worst."

"Best guess?"

"Well, if it was her and Carl then maybe there was a reason for a fight. We know how strong she is and if she was suspicious, that would give her a motive; far too early to tell."

"Why come back? That what was what she did in Portugal."

"Probably thought that no one heard. Certainly didn't expect us to still have a valid search warrant and spare keys."

"Plenty of time to have met up with the 'removal' people and make sure Carl was gone. Should have run when she saw the uniform outside but she was getting out of a cab and he was in the shadows. The rest of the team were on the floors above and below."

The Police—A Little Later

"So the two hours that were unaccounted for she was in the restaurant?"

"Yes, Sir, the waitress said she was in plain sight and only went to the loo once which was just as they were going to serve the food so they know it was only seconds not minutes."

"So what on earth was happening? The boyfriend who we suspect visits the flat with someone who looks like her, gets beaten up and then carried out in a wardrobe? That makes no sense at all."

"No, Sir, but we actually can't be sure it was him as there are no face shots and the quality is poor so we can't even do one of the checks where the way he walks is matched."

"Is there anyone else living there who might match the description, even two people who know each other who met by chance and walked home together, or even a dinner party. Have we talked to all the people who live in that block?"

"No, Sir, I was going to ask for authority to do that. There are fifty flats in total and by the nature we only get a few each visit, it's going to take a few days."

"Well, you had better get on with it. We don't have anywhere else to go at the moment."

"No, Sir, it's a mystery. It is as bad as the unsolved murder that is linked to the guy, so I now am thinking that he has disappeared either deliberately or he may have been abducted. Do you think that's possible?"

"Yes, it's an outside possibility. Are we sure it's his blood?"

"Yes, Sir, we had the DNA rushed through, it's his. So unless someone deliberately sprayed his blood on the walls and dripped it on a cushion, he was there, that is why we didn't look for a positive ID on the CCTV. He was there, the DNA confirms it."

"How sly or clever is this guy? Is he capable of faking his own kidnap?"

"I would say yes, but it's one thing agreeing with me and another getting any sort of proof."

"Get someone who is very good on scenario plotting and get them to imagine all the possibilities. We need to do a much more detailed analysis so we can look for specific clues. I feel we are being sold a dummy here somehow and it pisses me off that we seem to be being manipulated."

"Yes, Sir, and as soon as we have anything from the door to door, I will let you know."

"Good enough then. I have to brief upstairs now and they are going to be all over me if we don't find something soon."

Jane's Story

So Carl was in my flat according to the police. I have no idea how it happened, just that there was blood spattered over the walls and a bit dripped on a cushion. Luckily, I can prove that I was nowhere near when the supposed delivery of a wardrobe that was then removed again. They could not prove it went into my flat but someone had been there. Apparently, no footprints so they wore protective coverings.

Also Carl, it seems, has now disappeared. The police suspect that he is dead. They are pushing suicide it seems, remorse for the problems he caused.

Could he have been waiting in my flat and someone was following him? I know he could get a set of keys cut, he had that sort of contacts the police told me.

Uncle Bob and Mark the Vape

"Have we covered the tracks?"

"Yes, it's all well-hidden. The police will never find out what happened as long as we don't get another plonker like Tony."

Uncle George and the Boss

"What are we going to do with the bloke, Carl?"

"His trainer scam is quite impressive. We could copy it and apply it to a number of other products. It is legal and lucrative. We could employ him to keep him quiet. When he was under the drugs, he told us the full story from his side. He suspects his wife but felt he didn't have any alternative but to 'keep her on' in his words."

"He has five million in the bank and he can probably get about half that out without upsetting the wife, so we could employ him in another country and he would have no money worries."

"OK then make the offer, life or death. Make sure he knows it's us who did Tony so he is certain to stay on side. Oh and drop her a mobile, same as the one she used at the beginning. Let her know what is going to happen, but tell her we will be 'disposing' of Carl and are going to take half the money."

"When she has agreed, do the usual thing with the bank account switch so it's not traceable"

***

"Is he awake now, no drug's effect going on?"

"Yes, boss, he is fine. Asking if he can let that tart know he is OK. She, like everyone else, thinks he is dead. Cheeky sod, didn't want to contact his wife, just the tart!"

"If you want, he could send some sort of coded message."

"What do you mean?"

"Well, they met at the Galaxy hotel and he could say 'your meeting at the Galaxy hotel has had to be postponed, but rest assured, your meeting will be re-arranged. The venue will have to change, but we will be in contact at some time in the not too distant future'. Then sign it off with something they both recognise. She will know it's from him as it's the burner phone he bought."

"That is a good idea, George, do it, but make sure he knows how lucky he is."

Naomi's Story

Now the bastard Carl has disappeared. It seems from what the police are saying that he went to that tart's flat and had some sort of problem because there was his blood on her walls and furniture. Carl knows that she was framed for the murder. He might suspect but he does not know for certain I was involved.

But I have joint control over the accounts now, so I wonder what he was thinking going there?

Carl's Story

My head hurts and I can't see anything, it's pitch black. I seem to be tied up and in a chair. I thought it was a mugging when those two guys jumped me round the corner from the police station. Strange, the pain in my head does not feel like I have been hit, it's more like a hangover and nothing else hurts.

How long have I been out? Where am I and what on earth is going on?

Here they are again, handcuffs and a bag over the head. Are they going to execute me? I am bundled into the back of a van and handcuffed to the seat. The bag is off my head. I can't see out because it is all enclosed. At least, there is a seat and I am strapped in.

I can as well drink the water they have left for me. Judging by the way they treated me, I may live. They were careful and even asked if I wanted something to eat. I was too terrified to realise I was hungry.

The van stops once and the front doors open and close, and we set off again.

We have just pulled up; well this is face up time I guess. I have never prayed but I do now. The back door opens behind me and two different guys come in.

"Hi I am Peter and he is Alan. Now don't be difficult and you will be OK, understand?"

I say yes and nearly say 'sir' after. I could easily wet myself I am so scared. We get out and are outside a hotel in the countryside, rolling hills and very pretty.

"Come this way and carry that bag."

I realise that it is actually a suitcase that is mine; how did they get that? I bet Naomi allowed them to take it. We go in and register three rooms. Peter says no need for help to the rooms, so we go up. We go into 'my' room and beer is offered, which is a surprise.

Peter explains that I have been lucky and when the van stopped and he took over. His orders are to make me an offer, one that I would be rather stupid to refuse he says.

Well, that was a turn up! They kidnapped me, drugged me and now want me to work for them. I have to trust them as they are quite capable of killing me and are going to tell Naomi that I am being disposed of and let her draw her own conclusions.

I didn't like the way that they started the conversation by saying that they will be disposing of me. I thought I was going to die, instead I end up in a nice hotel drinking beer. If I had kicked off though, I probably would be dead.

I hope they don't just take the money and then get rid of me, but they are now talking about sending me abroad with a new identity. It's more like witness protection than kidnapping.

I am not stupid and I realise that the different levels of criminal that exist do work together. I even had my little group who would do 'work' and it is explained that with modern communications and the dark web, the transition from what I was doing that was close to illegal and things that are illegal is now quite a big thing, like building today where sub-contractors do most of the work and the 'employers' just manage and run 'projects'.

That way most people operate in a little 'bubble' and have no idea how bad or illegal an operation they are involved in, in case they get caught. Having experienced this now all the way from big operations that are worth protecting at any cost, having heard about the bloke who died, to these two who are 'trainers'.

So I spend a week with Peter and Alan learning my new role in life. It will be just like my old life but with a level of protection; no longer a sole trader in a market, but the head of a division of a semi-legal operation where I am doing nothing illegal and will not get into trouble. Then off we go to another location, private and very quiet.

Now my middle name is Edward and some of my mates used to call me Ed, and that is my new name. I get a new surname but they have chosen something to make me comfortable, which is sensible I suppose as I am now on their 'side'.

God, my head hurts. I was never cut out for languages and this lot have me learning Spanish and Portuguese. It seems that my new 'job' is that I am to co-ordinate the trainer sales and will need the basics at least. There are as well a couple of other 'products' that are going to use the same idea; cheap original product due for Africa or South America will get diverted and I will be organising the distribution.

I have already met my 'staff' and 'contacts'. Amazing how these guys operate. They have taken guys who were doing similar things and brought them together as a team. It's just like a big company who creates teams to complete projects and move staff around. Just that these guys are all close to being clever petty criminals who, like me, are offered the opportunity of a safe 'job'. No pension though I mention and that raises a laugh.

Jane's Story

Well, the flat is cleaned and I am just about functioning. What a nightmare. I could not have imagined anything worse that could have happened to me except physical damage. Who could have done such a thing. Well, I think I know. It's the people who set me up in the first place.

I thought for a while it was Carl who was jealous but it was his blood in the flat, so either he was killed or injured there.

Why would he go to my flat? The police don't know and he has never been there before. Yes, he had the address for emergencies like lost mobiles but we never met there. Was he stalking me I wonder. What a mess. I don't know what to do.

Jane and Mike

I have now made a plan. I am going to tough this out. I may decide on moving flats later but for now, I am going to get on with my life. I think a holiday would be in order once the next assignment is out of the way, probably a couple of months. This has taken a chunk out of my life, most of the summer, so I think some autumn sun in Greece or Turkey will be what I will do.

Oh now my newly returned phone is ringing.

"Hi, Jane, how are you?" It is my old friend, Mike, who I once worked with and still get the odd job through.

"I am fine. It's good to hear a friendly voice. Fancy a drink or some lunch?"

"I am up for that, just finished a report and am in need of a relax."

"The usual place about 12.30?"

"That's good. I will see you there in an hour. Some lunch and a glass will be perfect."

Mike and I spend lunchtime talking. He had no idea that I had been through so much. He did have one small project that he wanted to run by me but as soon as I had told him the outline of what had happened, he made a couple of calls to cancel meetings and we had a really good talk. It was great to be able to off load on someone who is a genuine friend.

We nearly had a thing a few years ago. The attraction was there but he is happily married, and we were sufficiently open to admit the attraction but to mutually decide it was not a good idea. I had actually met his wife separately and thought she seemed as genuine as he did, so he is one of the few people I trust. Funny that I didn't think of him earlier when I was in the depths of the mess, but I guess I would not have wanted to bother him with my problems.

"So you think that I could do most of my work from abroad? That's not a bad idea. I am fed up with this country rather and we can still do lunch once a month when I am back for meetings. Friends like you are what has kept me going. I know I could have been convicted if you and the others had not been in the bar and told the police."

It's funny I don't really trust the police now, they can get things so wrong. I have nearly been convicted of murder, kept in jail for allegedly harming a boyfriend and even now I don't feel I am free. It's like I am being watched.

"Yes, Mike, I think living abroad would be a good solution to the problem, thanks for your help."

We part on good terms, with a loose agreement that he will help me get more assignments and we will be sharing the proceeds so I will get a little less and he will start building some regular extra income that he will need when his lovely wife has to cut back on what she does.

It took nearly two hours of me talking about me before he dropped the bombshell that he will be a father in five months' time.

Naomi's Story

God, that was scary. I was out shopping and someone slipped a mobile, just like the one the private detective gave me, into my handbag.

When the text arrived, I didn't understand as it's not the same noise as my mobile makes. 'You will be called in an hour and are being watched so don't talk to anyone before we talk to you'.

I was scared witless. I sat in the car. I had left all the groceries in the supermarket and just walked out.

The call came and I recognised the voice, very matter of fact. "Your husband is being disposed of and if you don't want to join him, you will not make a fuss when half his money is withdrawn from the bank. The police will interview you and you will know nothing, which apart from this phone call, is true. You can keep the rest. It should be enough for the rest of your life and you can keep the business if you wish. Agree now."

I said yes as much out of fear as anything else and then dumped the phone in the same way as I had the first.

Poor Carl, he was not a really bad person; that it seems is me, I started this off. No, that is unfair on me. Carl stated this by having that girl on the side. I must keep this in perspective. I can't tell anyone but when the police decide Carl is dead, I can tell a good story than does not include me.

Will I have to identify the body I wonder. Oh no, I can feel the nightmares starting again just like when that girl was framed.

Detective Inspector Will Knowles

"Any news on the Carl bloke."

"No, Sir, he is still missing. We have had a few sightings from the bit on Crimewatch but none that has proved positive. The best sighting was when someone was seen on Southend pier, best visual match. We get the guy going on to the pier, looking woozy and weaving, and not coming off. So either he jumped, fell or managed to slip by somehow."

"How on earth did we let two and a half million leave his bank account when we were supposed to be watching it?"

"Sir, we only put a 'watch' and the money disappeared in a few minutes. It seems he had a special arrangement that allowed large sums to be transferred, not the usual 25,000. He did have to buy containers of stuff so it's not that much of a surprise."

"Well, we had better get on the trail and find where it's gone. At the moment, we have an unsolved disappearance, someone framed for murder and someone murdered, all connected and we have no idea how."

***

"What do you mean we can't trace the money?"

"Sir, the accounts that were credited were all overseas which was in fact normal for our man. The problem is that all the accounts that were credited were closed as soon as the money had been removed and that was minutes. This was a very slick operation and we are trying to chase the funds but they do seem to have disappeared."

"Some were bankers' drafts that are difficult to trace and some was even taken in cash, and all in countries where we can't really push for information because we don't have the best reciprocal agreements. Also the amounts of money are not enough for our money laundering guys to go after. It's almost like there is some organisation conspiring against us, not just one guy trying to disappear."

"Exactly when in time was this?"

"At exactly the same time as the sighting on Southend pier. So the theory I have is that whoever had him arranged to get hold of the money and then dumped him in the water, probably drugged."

Naomi's Story

"Madam, we want to know if you authorised the transfer of two point five million pounds to foreign bank accounts? Remember you are under caution and we are recording this. I am sure your solicitor here has told you how serious this is if you were complicit?"

"No, officer, I have no idea what happened. You can check the account. It's not one I use or even knew about until this whole thing blew up. Remember the letter Carl produced giving me access, well that was the first I had heard of it. Check my account, you will see all I do is buy the usual stuff, fuel and food mainly."

"Anyway, I want to know what has happened to my husband. He was in custody, you released him and he disappeared. Are you keeping him somewhere as your lot were the last to see him alive. I want some answers and my solicitor has a letter demanding information if you have it, give him the letter. Now can you sign that you have received it and can I go?"

"Yes, Madam, you can leave. I will pass this to my superiors for action and I am sure your solicitor will be in touch with us."

Well, that went well, better than I expected. That solicitor is a clever chap, having the 'attack' primed and thinking up the preposterous idea that the police were 'the last to see Carl alive'.

It certainly shook that detective constable who was asking the questions. Lucky it was not a more experienced copper.

Private Detective Steve Morris

I am not sure what has been going on but the newspapers have been all over the girl's case and the papers have speculated that there is a link to a murder in the midlands. I wonder if Naomi can shed any light?

Well, that was a waste of time. I tried to get her to talk, saying I had found a few extra notes that she could have and she completely blanked me, sounded rather frightened actually. Mind you that was how she sounded most of the time anyway.

I will call Mark the Vape and see if I can uncover anything.

"Mark, I wonder if you have heard anything about the guy who we were 'interested' in a few weeks ago? I passed one of your mobiles on to his wife and heard no more, apart from the few quid you gave me a week later."

"Steve, I suggest that you just leave it. The whole thing is in a different place now and best left alone, if you know what I mean."

Blanked twice so there will be something going on. I wonder if I can dig anything up that could make me a few quid.

Result—Carl has disappeared and the cops think he is in hiding, according to my special source. I wonder if he is still alive actually. These guys don't mess around. Lucky I am on the outside or I could get hurt!

So not only disappeared but run off with a bag full of dosh. I didn't think he had the connections. Yes, he had connections all over the world, but not good, or should I say bad enough to pull off that sort of stunt.

Private Investigator Steve Morris with Mark the Vape

"Mark, good to see you. Can I have a try of that special vape you mentioned, the one that has CBD oil in it?"

"Steve, you mean the spliff in a bottle, no problem. How come? You never touched the stuff before."

"Well, I have always wanted to give it a go but been scared of getting caught. I would lose my licence and I am quite partial to eating and the thought of sleeping rough never has appealed. But if you have it on display and feel safe, then who am I to ask questions."

"Here you go; twenty to you, thirty to everyone else."

"Thanks, mate. Now another bit of help. I need to get someone followed and they know me so I need some legs who can spend a couple of half days."

"What make do you need?"

"Pardon."

"Male or female, you twerp, also age and are they noticeable or not. You know like you can walk into a room and out and no one notices, because you are such a non-descript twat, your best asset; shame you never had the brains too!"

"You bastard, oh well if I can't take it then I would be in the wrong job. I think a bird would be best and not too noticeable, but not drab as there may be some posh places to visit."

"OK give me a day or so and I will get a few numbers for you."

Mark the Vape and Uncle Bob

"Hey, Uncle, the PI Steve has asked for some help and wants a tart to follow someone. No details but I thought you should know as he has been sniffing about I think, putting his nose where he should avoid?"

"Yes, Mark, that's right. I hear he has been asking questions and been trying to find that Carl bloke who, it seems, has disappeared with a large chunk of his cash."

"Well, that does surprise me. I wonder where he is hiding? Perhaps, somewhere in the Sussex downs. I hear the views are great and the accommodation is free to the properly connected people."

"Careful, Mark, too close to the knuckle. I hope you didn't let on to your old school chum about the 'car storage facility'."

"Of course not, I like breathing, don't I. So who shall I put his way, any ideas?"

"I know the ideal 'lady' so give me three phones and make a note of the numbers."

"What?"

"Mark, wake up, will you. Three phones and I need the numbers so you can give them to your mate. Now three ladies, Mary, Sharon, and shall we say, Chantal?"

"What?"

"Give me some sticky labels and write the numbers and names on the back of the phones, and have a note of them. Give them to Steve and I will give them to the lady who he will recruit. We don't want to have three people on standby, do we. The phone rings, she looks at the back and answers with the correct name, is that so hard?"

"OK, I get it now. God, you can be difficult at times, but that is clever enough. What shall I say about these three ladies?"

"Mary is the sensible one with fake glasses so she looks studious, Sharon is the typical Boots assistant and Chantel can do Essex or the Ritz."

"OK I have noted all that. Here are the phones, let's just call each one to make sure the sim cards are correct."

"Right, that's the third one then. I notice you didn't answer as Chantal!"

"Hahaha, and I don't mean any of that. Now bugger off and I will call Steve when you let me know you are ready. It's nearly closing time and I need to do the accounts."

"Accounts, Mark, you are getting posh!"

"Bob, these days hardly anyone uses cash so I don't 'cash up' like you had to in the middle ages when you were a lad."

"Mark, that is very cheeky, but I deserved it all. Now, I am off. Bye."

Steve Morris

So I am going to take on Mary who is one of the ladies who Mark put me in touch with.

We are meeting in a bar near Waterloo station and she says she will get going straight away.

Well, she was a good investment, seems to be very able and can follow people very surreptitiously. I even did a test and she managed to follow me for a mile and I never saw her. She is good. She simply popped off a hair band on that had dragged the hair from her face and had a reversible coat.

Simple but it changed her appearance completely. She showed me and it took about thirty seconds, very impressive.

I have asked her to follow Naomi for a day and if possible, make a contact with her. Then perhaps have a coffee by saying she will be back in the same place the next day. I followed Naomi for a while when I was supposed to be following Carl to make sure it was not her messing around.

It's amazing how some people live. Anyway, I have a list of her favourite supermarket, coffee shop and hairdresser. It will be a good place to start.

Mary Following Naomi

What a palaver. That woman didn't go to any of the places Steve mentioned. I had to catch her at home and follow her. Different supermarket, a pub rather than a coffee shop, still I managed to talk to her in the pub. I managed to get in before her when it was obvious where she was going. I was 'waiting for a bloke'. By texting Mark, he called me and 'cancelled' the drink we had arranged and I was 'quite upset', and Naomi was quite sweet but didn't let anything slip.

I followed her all day and she only went to her husband's old office and back home after the pub. I wonder if there is any chance of a phone tap. Probably best not to as the police are still sniffing around I hear.

Mark and Mary

"Mary darlin', I have just come off the phone with Uncle George and we have a treat for you. How do you fancy making ten grand more?"

"Mark, you could call me by my real name you know. Anyway, I am always ready for that sort of money as long as my legs stay crossed. What do you need doing? I guess it is Steve who need some sort of kicking, though ten grand is more like disposed of."

"Well not quite disposed of, but if he dies; not traceable to you, but you will have to give him a nice cocktail and a nudge down some steps."

"What am I feeding him then?"

"Nothing lethal, but enough to make him groggy. Then a simple trip should do it."

Mary

Mark was pretty upset. He suspected that Steve had gone off piste and it was easy to confirm. My report to Steve is in a day or so, meeting at the same pub. I will be following him from his place but he will not know as I need to know where he parks his car.

I have to dress up like another woman as well and try and walk a bit like her. I have the picture and a few quid to get the right clothes. Lucky, I already have what they asked for and even have the correct makeup that will make me a close copy of her. I wonder if they chose me because I look like her; same build and I have to wear a wig to disguise myself.

Mary and Private Investigator Steve

"Hi, Steve, mine is a white wine spritzer with soda."

"Wow, Mary, I didn't recognise you. You do look familiar though. I can't remember who it is you look like."

"Well, maybe it's because you did tell me to change my appearance so I would not get clocked."

"Thanks for that. I have the file here for you. It's all on this memory stick so you can look at it later. Is that ok?"

"Yes, love, it's fine. I didn't want to have too much really, so can you let me know how it went?"

"It was a piece of cake apart from the time it took following. That Naomi was not as predictable as you told me, so there is an extra half-day to pay for."

"That's is not a problem. I will pass you the envelope under the table. It's got the original fee in it and I will have to go to the cashpoint to get the rest. Do you know where the nearest is?"

"No, sorry, but there will be one in Waterloo. We can walk over when I have given you the verbal report."

Description of Following Naomi

"OK well, that all seems fine. She is not doing anything suspicious so I can let that line of enquiry go."

"I would offer you another drink but I feel a bit rough. I might be getting a cold, so let's get that money and say au revoir."

Mary's Story

Well, that was easy enough; slipped the potion into his drink when he got me mine and a gentle nudge when we were at the top of the steps outside Waterloo. He went down quite hard and I legged it off and took his car. The nudge was when I picked his pocket for the keys.

I changed in the loo and watched as the police and then the ambulance came. He seemed to be semi-conscious when they put him in.

Mark and 'Mary'.

"Mark, here are his keys. It's the blue Freelander in the car park down the street as you asked. I also came the route you asked for. Why did you want me to come that way?"

"Because there are no cameras apart from the car park. You did use the proper face covering, didn't you?"

"Yes, of course, any camera will think its him if anyone looks."

"Did you get the business cards I asked for?"

"Yes, here they are. I used gloves in the car and on them. Here is a spare glove so you can handle them."

"Thanks, Mary, you are a gem. I do have some somewhere but had forgotten to get them as I would be handling 'evidence'. Did you get anything with DNA on it?"

"Yes, here is a piece of chewing gum from his ashtray and the fork he used when we were in the pub. You can just wipe the handle across the card I think."

"Yup, all sorted then, thanks. Take care. Here is you fee."

"Plain brown envelope, how criminal!"

"Well, we do like a laugh, don't we?"

"Yes, you are a fun guy to work with. How come you never ask me for a drink?"

"Because of business and pleasure, sorry we have to behave or we get points deducted like Steve Morris who used up all his and look what happened."

"At least, he is still alive."

"Only for the moment, I wanted the business cards as a backup, keep very shtum."

"Point taken then."

"Bye, Mary."

Private Investigator Steve Morris

"Thank you, nurse. I still feel rather groggy but you can ask that policeman to come in now."

"Good morning, Sir. I trust that you are feeling up to this interview."

"Yes, officer, I am not quite all here, but I want to get it all over with. I don't remember much of what happened. I was at Waterloo and fell down the steps is all I know."

"Well, Sir, it seems that you have been lucky, that fall would have killed most people, or at least some severe broken bones. That is why I am here. How did you manage to fall and not get hurt, it is almost as if you were drugged."

"I was feeling rather woozy. I had only had one pint so that was not it. Maybe the pasty I had with it was off."

"Might have been, Sir, so you were feeling under the weather. So perhaps the first bump on the head was enough to put you out so not being tense saved you."

"Yes, officer, thank you, it does explain things. I was very lucky."

"At the top of the steps on the CCTV, there was a woman just behind you, quite close. Who was she? Were you together?"

"No, officer, don't know who you are talking about."

That was a bit close, the last thing I needed was the fuzz sniffing around. I will have a look at Mary's report when I get back. They say they are going to let me out later, just a few bruises, so lucky.

"Nurse, I forgot to tell that policeman that my car is still in the car park, can you catch him please."

"No need. They must have realised and found it as someone dropped your keys in while he was here. Not another one in uniform, just a plain clothes guy. He said your car was back at your flat, very organised."

At the Police Station—DI Will Knowles and DS Fred Wills

"Did the uniform fool him? We don't want him to know we are suspicious until we are certain."

"I think so, no mention of the woman, but he could have been lying."

"Did the CCTV definitely show the woman pushing him?"

"Not that we could use for a prosecution but enough for us to look further. Who was she?"

"I have sent the picture round and may have something. She looked very like someone 'of interest' in that case of the guy who died twice."

"You had better get in touch then set up a meeting and we will hand this over."

"Did we manage to get a blood sample for analysis?"

"Yes, we did at the lab now. We told the hospital that we needed to make sure he was not under the influence of any drugs, which is true. Only thing is that we didn't have his permission."

Detective Inspector Will Knowles and Detective Sergeant Fred Wills

"Do we have the blood test back yet?"

"Yes and here's a thing, Rohypnol in his system, enough to make him groggy and easy to push over."

"How sure can we be that this is that girl Jane doing the pushing?"

"It's very like her, face is covered mostly. Build seems to be the same. The quality of the pictures is not good, but there are items of clothing that match the style she wears."

"So another search of her apartment for the clothes and do we bring her in?"

"Yes to the search. First ask if she has the clothes and ask her if she has worn them recently. Look at the clothes and try to see if there is anything that will place her there and does she have an alibi for the time of the alleged assault."

Phone Call to Jane from the Police

"Good morning, miss, it's Detective Constable Burton. We have been trying to ascertain what has been happening and may have some progress. Is there any chance I could drop in and check a few details?"

"Yes, of course. The place is a bit of a mess but not as bad as when the blood was everywhere, just a bit of a jumble. I am trying to work but can spare half an hour. When?"

"How about I come over now. It will just be me and Detective Constable Susan Howe, is that OK?"

"Yes, of course. I will put the kettle on."

At Jane's Flat

"Good afternoon, miss, how are you doing?"

"I am OK, still very confused about what is going on but if I can help, what do you need to know?"

"Well, miss, there has been an assault, someone we know is involved and we have suspicions as to why this happened. Now do you own clothes like the ones in this picture? It's just for elimination purposes at the moment."

"Yes, I do have some similar items. I don't think I have worn them recently though. Why are you asking?"

"As I said, just elimination purposes. Could you show them to DC Howe please. I don't need to be present in case there are any items that might embarrass you in front of a male."

"No problem, come this way, DC Howe, they are in the spare bedroom wardrobe."

"Miss, can we take these and show DC Burton please. They do match the items exactly."

"So, miss, we now have a bit of a dilemma. Can I show you this picture please, it is of a woman that looks quite like you."

"Yes, that looks like me but why are you asking?"

"We will get to that in a moment. Can you tell me where you were three days ago between noon and 2.00 pm?"

"I was here working."

"Can anyone confirm that?"

"Now look here, Sergeant, this is getting a bit heavy. Am I under suspicion? I thought you just wanted to check a few details and now you are asking me for an alibi. What am I supposed to have done this time? Murdered someone else? I don't think I want to say anything else until I have a legal representative present."

"OK, miss, then I will have to ask you to come down to the police station and we will arrange for someone to be with you. Would you like the same person as last time if they are free?"

"Are you arresting me!"

"Will you come voluntarily please, miss, just until we get this resolved."

"No, I won't. I am feeling harassed and this will be the third time I have had to put up with your unreasonable behaviour."

"Oh dear miss, in that case, Jane Adams, I am arresting you in connection with an aggravated assault that happened at approximately 13.00 last Monday which resulted in the victim being taken to hospital with potentially life threatening injuries. Failure to mention…"

Jane's Story

"So here I am again! Innocent of any crime but being blamed for what they are telling me could be attempted murder."

"Yes, miss, we understand how you feel, but you have seen the picture that looks like you and the victim is known to have been employed by Carl's wife and has probably followed you in the past and was one of the key people that started this matter. Now you say you don't know the victim but we can't be sure that is true at the moment. Why would anyone harm this person?"

"He may have many enemies but we do know that he has been investigating you, and that gives you reason to hold at least a grudge against him. Have you any answer for that?"

"Look, I don't know him. I have just been arrested for the third time and you had to let me go the first two because I was innocent."

"Miss, we let you go because there was compelling evidence that you were not involved. You could still have had knowledge of the crimes that have been committed and I have to remind you that one is the murder of a man that you had a relationship with, however brief, a few days before he died."

"Can they do this? Can they hold me when they have no actual proof?"

"As your solicitor, I suggest that you do as much to help. There is obviously an agenda here but at the moment, we don't know what that is. Do you wish for us to have a private conversation to try and resolve these matters?"

"Actually no, how long can you hold me before I am either charged or released?"

"I will answer that, miss. We arrested you at approximately 2.30 pm today. We are allowed to keep you in custody for twenty-four hours. We will apply for an extension while we pursue other lines of enquiry and that can be up to ninety-six hours, or four days."

"Back in the cell now, trying to hit that policeman was not a good thing to do, but I just lost it. I have been under so much pressure and I have that assignment to complete by the end of next week. God knows what damage this could do if it comes out that I didn't finish it because I was locked up. But I can't help them. It's just like before, someone is trying to frame me and I have no idea why."

Detective Inspector Donald Jones

"Jane Adams, we have decided to release you, but request that you stay in London and will retain your passport. The incident with the officer you assaulted has been dropped. However, if you ever do that again you will be charged with assault."

Jane's Story

So here I am again sort of free. Why did they let me go again if I am a suspect? I have to admit that the CCTV did look like me. I think in court they would have to do some sort of analysis, like the way I walk, but I am pretty devastated. I was so looking forward to that free trip too. I wonder if that can be put off until the police have cleared me.

Oh God, what if I am charged again. I am not sure I can take too much more of this.

But at least I can finish that assignment now and no one will be the wiser.

Private Detective Steve Morris

Well, that was a bit of a strange thing to happen. Was I pushed down the stairs like the police seem to think? I don't know if Mary had anything to do with it. She was a way behind me when it happened. We had said that we didn't want any CCTV showing us together, but she could have speeded up? The cops are being very tight lipped. I tried to find out if they were still investigating and hit a stone wall.

Anyway, I am going to look at all the information again, but I don't think there is anything that I can gain from looking to get anything from anyone.

I am going to drop it now. I have the enquiry about a husband is cheating with the well-endowed wallet walker; what a change. Still I have to put the beer on the table so I am off to reconnoitre the guy's house and get his car details so I can start to track him.

Nice house. I think my rates have just gone up a bit. Odd though, I think I know him from somewhere, just a vague recollection of the face. Probably from checking up on guys from the same golf club. That area seems rife with guys looking for something a bit younger and firmer. He is apparently going away for a golf trip according to the barman at his club, leaving Friday mid-day it seems. That was worth the twenty quid. I will be waiting outside by 11.00 so I don't miss him.

So here I am and I don't know what words to use. They are mostly swear words as I arrived here at 11.00 and his black Range Rover was gone. Must have left early. I will wait till noon in case it's in the garage, but it would be the first time the lazy sod had put it away since I have been watching.

Well well, he has just driven past with the blonde in the passenger seat. He must have popped to collect her. Some nerve driving past his house. What if his missus had spotted him?

Off we go then. I wonder where they are off to? Easy to follow as he is quite the slow and polite driver. She has probably got her hand on his dick so he is having to concentrate hard. No pun intended.

Well, we are about fifty miles away, mostly small roads too. I suppose no cameras just in case.

This lane is pretty disgusting, so much mud and cow 'stuff', slippery as hell and now he has speeded up. I hope he does not meet a tractor coming the other way.

Police in Kent

"So what happened from your perspective, Mr Partridge."

"Someone stole my tractor and drove it off. I was doing the big hay bales with the big spike to lift them."

"Did you leave the keys in the vehicle?"

"Yes and the engine was running as I was struggling to get the bale to drop off, so I got out to lever it. I was half way through when the tractor was backed up and the bale fell on me. I pushed it off, lucky I didn't get a broken leg, and ran after it."

"Could you see who it was?"

"No, I suspect one of those travellers. They were grubby looking, but they could certainly drive the tractor, not their first time."

"I am surprised that you didn't catch them as they had to turn round."

"No, I couldn't. I ran across the yard but slipped and fell, I did hurt my arm then, hence the sling."

"Thank you, Mr Partridge, can you arrange to get to the station sometime to give a statement please."

"Do I need to, officer? I have told you everything."

"Sorry, Sir, but remember the person in the car died with your spike through him, so it's manslaughter probably. Yes, theft as well but that is pretty insignificant when you consider. Can you make it early tomorrow? I can arrange a car if needed."

"No, officer, I am sorry, I was being selfish, that poor man. I can get my wife to bring me in tomorrow, about 9.30, if that's OK? I need to sort the cows out before I come in and I will be doing it one handed."

"That will be fine, Sir. I will arrange for someone to be available to take the statement."

"When will I get my tractor back?"

"When forensics have been over it with a fine tooth comb. We will have to keep the spike as it is close to a murder weapon."

"I understand. I can borrow one from the next farm if my arm gets better before I get the tractor back. The idiot who stole it should never have gone on the road. It is against the law, I read it recently. If I remember correctly, its Section 40 of the Road Traffic Act. I only remember because I read it on my 10th birthday, what a thing to remember."

"Sir, I suggest that you put that in your statement as it shows that you know the rules, it will help you avoid any repercussions. Not fair I realise as you have no blame attached, but in these politically correct times, you can't be too careful."

Police Station in Kent

"So what did the forensics guys find at the scene?"

"Not much, Sir. The tractor steering wheel and seat had been wiped clean and the pedals had plastic bags put on them so no trace could be left; really carefully done. Not really the style of travellers as we first suspected, but no evidence there at all."

"If that's the case, we had better give the tractor back, so nothing to go on then?"

"Not at the scene, Sir, but at the yard we did find something. There was a trip wire across the yard where the tractor had passed. There was a clever mechanism that meant that the tractor could drive over but someone catching the wire underneath would be tripped. So someone was being quite deliberate here."

"Sorry, but are you saying that this was a sophisticated theft that needed planning and careful execution?"

"Yes, Sir, it seems that it was almost military in its execution. I don't know how to describe it really. Tractor stops and the farmer gets out, the thief gets in and at the same time, two others erect the trip wire. They could not have done it earlier as the farmer might have noticed or tripped; beats me."

"As well the person driving the tractor jumped out still with the plastic bags on their feet and went on a circuitous route up to the car twice it seems, there were a few other tracks in the mud around and it could be that a vehicle stopped to pick them up, but again no proof."

"Why would they walk up to the pickup vehicle twice and why go to Morris's car. I suppose, to make sure he was dead?"

"Yes, that must have been it, Sir. He didn't touch the car as far as we can tell. We are pretty certain and he would hardly be likely to want to put something in the damaged vehicle, would he?"

"No, and now you have worried me. Look at this from a timing perspective. Why steal the tractor at that point in time, especially if you are taking the precautions that they took. A possible scenario is to take the tractor at that exact point in time and ensure that the owner is incapacitated, perhaps he was lucky to hurt his arm so he could not pursue these thieves as it looks like they may have been planning to get the driver of that particular car. Who was the guy?"

"A private detective with a record of never having broken the law but had come very close. A number of formal complaints, none ever upheld."

"Well, that does make it very fishy. We need to do this very carefully. We may have a murder on our hands."

"That was well spotted, Sir, I see what you mean. I didn't see it that way at all."

"You were too close to the evidence, it was when you laid it all out that the different scenarios became evident; still not certain, but enough to take up a level. Will you prepare and sign the paperwork? It won't do you any harm if the DCI sees your name on it."

"Thanks, Sir, I will. Do you want me to put in the different scenarios that you have identified?"

"Yes, and you can mention my name then. Don't want you taking all the glory, but well collated. Have we circulated the information in case the victim has anything we should know going on?"

"Yes, Sir, we have had one reply from the Met. I was about to ask if they can visit tomorrow quite early. The victim was known to them and had recently been the victim of an assault. They were very cagey. It sounds as if there is something going on that might explain why and what we are investigating."

Police Station in Kent

Detective Inspector Donald Jones from the Met and the Two Kent Detectives

"So tell me what happened. It sounds bizarre that our joint victim can get drugged with Rohypnol, pushed down some significant steps, end up in hospital and then get killed a week later."

"Yes, Sir, it does, and if we had not seen the small bits of evidence like the trip wire and the bags on the tractor pedals, we would have assumed that this was just an unlucky occurrence. Indeed at the beginning we did think that. It was only when forensics found the bags that we started probing deeper."

"Is there anything that I can use to trace the perpetrators? So far we have had a murder in the midlands that is linked as well, what is going on?"

"Can you push locally and see if there is anything that can be added please."

"Of course, Sir. We will keep your team informed either way in a couple of days. The burner mobile we found in the victim's car might give us something. It has had a few calls recently and we have tracked it so it shows us his route."

Uncle George and the Boss

"So is the potential leak plugged?"

"Yes, pretty much. No chance that there will be comeback this time as they won't get a clue."

"What avenues will they follow?"

"We have planted information so that they will go after Jane and Naomi. They are the closest that they will get as one employed that stupid private dick. Who did he think he was? He didn't know how the organisation works but he knew it existed."

"I almost feel sorry for that Jane. Here she is caught up in something that is not really her fault, other than she should keep her knickers on when men are married. It seems almost unfair to put her in the frame for another murder."

"Keep an ear open, let me know how things develop. One small worry is that Jane. We have Carl in training, he will be off in a few weeks so we don't want any repercussions. He will need to know that these two women are ok. Have we asked him about these two? What is your judgement as to how he would react if anything major happened to them?"

"Honestly don't know. He was cheating on his wife and didn't seem to care, but he did want to make sure she was ok, set up financially and so on, so he is not a complete bastard. Shall we simply ask him?"

"No, we don't ask, we tell. I see three possible scenarios. One is that one or both of the women are prosecuted and might go down for a crime they didn't commit; next, we can ensure that they don't, easy to leave a clue or two if the plods do move in that direction; last, does he want to see that Jane again? We have offered her that free holiday, so perhaps there could be some connection there."

"Do we know what she thinks of the plods? She has been a suspect in two murders now and that can't have been easy for her."

"No, we don't really know what she is thinking. When she is questioned again, shall we try and get the brief to ask the question? Our 'charity' can be concerned, can't it?"

"How do you do that, boss? 'Charity' is a wonderful word for our way of moving people around, even if they don't want to. Do you remember that guy who fancied himself as a DJ and we got him out to Croatia for the summer so the plods would forget about him? What a wanker he was. Three months in a campsite and he thought it was wonderful."

"He is back here now doing odd jobs for us but still goes back every year. The campsite love him as he is so cheap, and he loves it because there is always a grateful granny or two. Actually, maybe you are right, should we be getting proper charity status?"

"Do you want an answer to that?"

"No, boss, sorry I got carried away there. I will get the options given to Carl by the end of the week. I am picking up a punter from Gatwick on Thursday so he can have a spin in his car. I will get the team down there to add the questions to the part of the course where we teach people like Carl how far they can go and the consequences of crossing us."

"Is that the bit where we cut one of their fingers off?"

"No, boss, we don't do that really, we only pretend but frighten them so they don't cross us."

"I do like the expressions when they are shown the severed finger, don't you?"

"No, boss, I don't. I see the need for discipline but to pretend to cut someone's finger and then show them a fake with blood dripping off. They don't know it's not theirs as they know the anaesthetic we pretend we give them will numb the pain."

"I know. I was the one who thought that up, it works a treat. How many faint when we show them remind me?"

"About one in five pass out completely, and you are right, we don't really need to do it to Carl, but we will let him see it happen to someone else. He already knows that the man previously known as 'Tony' had to be dispatched. Why have there been so many stupid people on this job? We will be losing money at this rate."

"We will struggle to break even yes, but there is the benefit of Carl's clever import scam which will make us a few pounds. By the way, well done for spotting that. Apart from the trainers, are there any more ideas about these 'imports'?"

"Yes, boss, we are looking into phones and ladies shoes. Not the top brands, but the second tier, stuff that is just above the own brands from Marks and Sparks. We did look at bras."

"I bet you did."

"No, we had some of the stuff they sell in Africa sent over and their body shapes are so different. It's not that there are no ladies who would not buy them, but there is just not the demand."

"What about Eastern Europe or South America?"

"We are still looking at them. It takes time to get the products over at sensible cost. We don't want to alert anyone to the opportunity."

"OK, are we done? Actually, there is one more thing. Did the business cards with the burner mobile number that got planted on Morris get to Jane's flat and Naomi's house?"

"Yes, boss, and I will let you know when anything happens and an update in a week in any case."

Naomi's Story

Here we go again, police at the door.

"What do you want then? I hope you have brought some information about my husband?"

"No, Madam, we wonder if we could ask a couple of questions please?"

"OK but be quick, I am busy. I have a lot to learn about my potentially late husband's business and this is adding a lot of stress when I don't need it. Do I need my solicitor here?"

"I can't answer that, Madam, it is quite simple. Do you recognise the man in this picture?"

"Yes, he is the private detective that discovered that my husband was cheating on me. Why?"

"Thank you, Madam. I am sorry to tell you this but he was murdered yesterday and we have reason to believe you have information regarding his death. Can you tell us anything at all?"

"No, I can't. I have not seen him for weeks. You have been keeping an eye on him so why do you think I am involved. I think I should call my solicitor."

"Well, Madam, we do know that a phone call was made to the deceased and the triangulation of the mobile that made the call gives us reason to believe that it was made from this area. Given that this is quite rural, what are the chances of someone else other than yourself making that call?"

"I didn't make the call. Here is my mobile, check it!"

"The call came from a mobile that is not traceable, a pay as you go, so yes anyone could have made the call but the probability is that it was you. Do you have another mobile at all?"

"No, I don't, so please leave. I have had enough of this harassment. Go on get out!"

"Sorry, Madam, we are going to have to ask you to come to the station and we will get a warrant to search the premises here and your offices."

"I am not saying another word. Are you calling my solicitor or am I? Anyone would think this is a bloody police state!"

"Feel free to call. Are you going to come to the station or do I have to arrest you?"

"Oh I don't care, arrest me if you want but can I talk to my solicitor first so he is there when I get there. I am not having you lot harassing me into telling you what you want to hear."

"Scott, can you meet me at the police station. They want to question me under caution again and I am not at all happy. Thanks see you there."

"Thank you, Madam, it will look better that we didn't have to arrest you should anything come of this."

Jane's Story

"Hello, is that Jane Adams? This is the police regarding the incident where we discovered that you may have been involved in the assault on Steve Morris. Is it OK to ask a few questions?"

"Yes, it is, but please tell me everything is OK. I can't stand what is happening."

"Sorry, Jane, but we have a team outside your flat and I am only calling to say please let them in. Steve Morris was murdered yesterday and we have evidence that links you to that. We have a solicitor on standby for you if you will please come to the station."

"I will let them in but please, I can't take much more of this. What is happening?"

Detective Sergeant Fred Wills and Detective Constable Susan Howe

"How was she? She sounded in a dreadful state."
"She was on the couch, head in hands, sobbing away."

Jane's Story

Here I am in custody again. It seems a phone call was made from a pay as you go, burner, mobile from where I live and that mobile that was called was found in the wreckage of Steve Morris car after he had some sort of accident or attack. They are being very guarded.

I don't have the burner mobile that made the call, and I certainly have not had that Steve Morris round to leave a business card with the mobile number they found. How did a business card get down the back of my sofa? Someone must have broken in and planted it so that I would look guilty again. I swore they were wrong but they seem to believe I was involved somehow.

I can see a pattern. There is someone out there protecting themselves from the police and getting people killed to hide. So far Tony who didn't die in Portugal, Carl who has disappeared, presumed dead and now Steve Morris, who is dead. There must be something really bad or valuable out there for three people to die. Although, I suppose its two as Carl's body has not been found.

DI Donald Jones and Detective Constable Susan Howes

"Well, Sir, she denies everything and her brief has pointed out that we don't have any actual proof, just very clear circumstantial evidence."

"OK what about Naomi? It looks like she was involved as well?"

"Yes, Sir, exactly the same evidence and the same defence. Both women claim they know nothing. You know we found an identical business cards from Morris at Naomi's house with the burner number written on the back."

"Yes, I did and the fact that the two scenarios are identical seem suspicious. Do either of them have alibis?"

"No, Sir, only that they were at their respective residences when the calls were made and both of them deny having any phones other than the ones we know about."

"Any chance of tracing the sim cards?"

"Again no, Sir. They are part of a consignment that should be in a warehouse. We are getting the company to check if they are still there. I will report back when we have the three sim cards traced."

"OK keep me posted. This is just going round in circles and it will look like we are harassing these women if we don't get something solid soon."

"Yes, Sir."

Naomi's Story

That went better. They can't prove anything and my brief has warned them off. They will still be watching me, he suggested that the card could have been one left and the number on the back was a mistake by the PI. It sounded quite plausible when he explained it all and that the card in the bin was thrown because I didn't need him any more with Carl gone and me set up with the business.

That is going well too. The contacts were all on Carl's computer and when the police brought it back, they had taken the password off, stupid lot.

I have phoned all the suppliers and the sales contacts and am selling the contents of the two containers in the warehouse and have arranged for a couple of repeats, so I don't have to get anything new set up. Always a market for trainers on the markets.

I do need to start looking at adverts and the web sites so I see what is coming up. It will be fun to order a new line myself and really get a handle on this. There is so much money to be made and no one is disadvantaged, just the posh brands get a lower margin. They over charge so much in the UK I get discounts as well as if I am an African wholesaler and that means I can sell them at less than the retailers here can buy them.

I am almost tempted but if the likes of Nike discovered what was happening, they would tighten things up. I wonder how that husband of mine managed to think it up. It was probably when he went to Thailand before we met I don't think he went for trainers, but he did tell me he bought several pairs that he brought back. He was also truthful that he also brought back a few personal germs too, nothing that penicillin could not sort out.

He had tests done to prove it before we got married which was one of the things that helped. He seemed so honest. Now he is probably dead; oh that makes me sad again.

Ah well, at least I should be shot of the cops now.

Carl's Story

Well, this is nice. I have been here for two months now. This is one of the places where they hold the cars for the people wanting to avoid tax, so it is secure and virtually no one ever visits. Those who do, always have an appointment so I hide away when that happens, except for the ones I might meet again.

My ability to speak languages is certainly improving fast. Every day there is an hour of Portuguese or Spanish, as that is where I will be based to handle the car sales. They are still working on how to adapt my trainer 'business plan', as they call it, to be useable over there, so there are business meetings from time to time. It is quite strange, having 'business meetings' with people who I know are involved with what is on the edge of organised crime.

I have been told that I will be off in a month to my new home, which looks amazing. I can't wait to get there, as to be frank, it's boring here. I need more to do.

All I do is learn about the business, have all the paperwork rules explained and documented ready for when I am over there. It's not difficult given my experience with import and export, but I am itching to get on with it.

One of the good bits of not leaving here for three months is that the police have more or less given up on finding my body, as they assume I have been disposed of. That is leaving the girls in a bad place, I wonder if I should do something about it. I will talk to someone.

Having my finger prints altered hurt a lot, but the skin grafts seem to have taken well. Apparently, it is unlikely that my DNA will be taken unless I do something stupid, and that would be stupid as I would die soon after. These guys don't mess around and I have had it explained very clearly that if ever I am arrested, I will not likely survive long as no one is allowed to know what I know.

Not that I know much, I only know first names of these guys. Marina is my language coach, no idea if that is her real name but she answers to it whoever calls her. Dave is the guy teaching me about cars so I can appear knowledgeable;

some of the clients like the idea that I know about cars so they trust me more. They both take turns with the administration, how to use their special programs and how to secure the laptop so that the police can't get to the 'real' stuff should it ever fall into their hands.

I have met a couple of the Spanish and Portuguese customers too. They come over and drive their cars that they can't have until the tax they would pay drops right down. That is the scam here; very posh cars looked after and stored in lovely warm units until they are ready to be sent overseas. I get to drive the car out of the storage unit and then sit with and chat to the owner as they take their test drive.

Some of them are a bit dodgy but they are not actually breaking any laws, apart I suppose from the money laundering side; not sure how close to the knuckle that is. I believe I get that lesson in a day or two.

I do also get the lovely job of cleaning the car after its trip around our track. Up on the lift, a bit of steam and a few cleaning cloths for the underneath and then the coachwork specialist gives it the once over so the bodywork is like new. They do attention to detail very well and not just the cars, the whole organisation is very well oiled.

I do get to do the vacuuming as well, but as we get into the car indoors and never get out, there are barely a strand to pick up.

I expect the other staff here will be glad to see the back of me as when we have a meal together, I can't help myself telling anecdotes which generally make them wince. I was warned about that as once I am away from here, my past has to be the one they are teaching me. I am not banned from my past but have to be very careful.

I may be able to recruit some of the people who will work with me. I am still working on who I would trust. There are lots of people in my past and I am struggling to think of one with a tongue that can be kept still after a few drinks. Comes with the old territory I suppose. They were all what could be called 'wide boys', genuine characters from 'Only fools and horses' just like Dell Boy but with a rather nastier streak if pushed.

As I said, I was relating that over dinner the other night, I did get a laugh but not much of one.

One of the guys I knew did the Peckham water scam. He 'won' a load of plastic bottles with the ready to put on tops that 'clicked' when you unscrewed them. Filled them from the tap at the local public toilet a couple of dozen at a time and placed them with the market stalls to sell for 25p each. He sold the whole five thousand in a few days and made himself just shy of a grand. I am not sure if the laugh was for the association with Dell Boy or making money from what was called 'toilet water'.

Two months now and my language skills are much better. I am allowed the news on television and the newspapers.

Jane has been having a very bad time, worse now, framed now for the murder of the PI who caught us together; that was nine months ago.

I have asked to speak to a 'boss' as I think it is time that Jane was cleared. It must be draining to be constantly harassed. They used my blood to incriminate her and I want some sort of payback. I understand that they must, as an organisation, be kept under the radar and that is in my interest now.

Wow, I am being taken out, in the back of a van admittedly, but the other side of London. Apparently, I am going to be 'seen' and leave proof that I am still alive.

The 'boss' said, "You had better be worth it, mate. This will cost and be difficult to pull off." I said that with their organisation, it should be easy. Now I have to find some way of getting Naomi and Jane off the hook for the PI. Apparently, the daft bugger started to try and get that little bit more and that could have exposed the organisation.

What a group though. A few really bad people, but not rough like you expect gangsters to be, very organised and I can't believe the resources they have. They can get someone to do almost anything, even silencing possible leaks that would expose their existence.

They have burglars who will break into places, place evidence for the police to find, like they did in Jane's, twice; once it was my blood! Then again leaving the business card with the burner phone number. The boss told me these little bits to reassure me that I can be looked after, in more ways than one. If I step out of line, I am dead, but as long as I stay in line, then I will be looked after. I have to earn my keep and they will make profits from what I do, so it is in my interest to not let anyone know what is going on.

I will have an apparently legitimate business and be a cog in an organisation that looks after you in return.

I have even been told how I can leave alive, which is nice. If I come across a new opportunity, that is completely kosher and I want to go into it, then for a small interest they will help set it up and find someone to replace me. They seem to have some sort of human resources part of the organisation and that keeps an eye on potential rouges and also sources the sub contract people who provide tools, electronic stuff.

I am due two phones it seems, one UK and one Portuguese but I am warned not to have any personal numbers on them apart from the ones they approve.

Naomi's Story

Well, that was dreadful. Now I am being accused of helping kill the PI I employed. They even found a business card with a pay as you go number in a rubbish bin in the house, not Carl's office at home. I can't go in there yet. I am still so sad and want to know what happened to him.

I think my grief is worse because how do you grieve for someone who might not be dead, despite the blood they found in that woman Jane's flat.

The threat of suing for damages certainly got the polices' attention, so glad my solicitor is so on the ball.

Detective Inspector Will Knowles and Detective Sergeant Fred Wills

"So we got a confirmed sighting?"

"Yes, Sir, we had a tip off from someone who saw the picture on the wall and then saw Carl. It was at the motorway services so we pulled all the CCTV and it certainly looked like him."

"So we have definite proof that he is alive?"

"Yes, Sir. He bought a sandwich and sat and ate it on a bench, then threw the wrapper into a bin. Luckily, the bin was emptied just before and we were able to retrieve the contents and his DNA was on the wrapper and the bottle of coke he bought as well."

"So we know he is alive and presumably we have the CCTV of which car he got into?"

"There is a problem there, Sir. He got into a van and we did get the number."

"Great, so we can trace him."

"Sorry, Sir, no. Do you remember the van from earlier that was the same number as a police van well the same has happened again. This was running on fake plates and the real van was in a police station near Newcastle at the time."

"I don't believe it. Do you mean that we have lost him again?"

"Yes, Sir, it seems that the van pulled off at the next exit and was not picked up on ANPR anywhere."

"Do you mean we can't trace where it came from or where it went?"

"Afraid not, Sir, it is seen just before joining the motorway two junctions down, once on the motorway and then when it left, almost as if it was meant to happen."

"I don't believe this. So someone puts Carl in a van with a cloned police number plate, drives him to a motorway services, lets him be seen and then the van is seen leaving the motorway and never again?"

"Yes, Sir, that is pretty much it."

"You have to be kidding me. So the van is either driven avoiding cameras to the motorway or the plates are changed just prior to its arrival, the scenario happens and then they avoid cameras or change the plates again?"

"Yes, it does seem bizarre but that is what happened. We even looked for similar vans that could have had their plates changed, but nothing, not even a similar van. It just disappeared."

Mark the Vape and Uncle Bob

"How did the show go?"

"Well, Mark, the set up was good, thanks. Those camouflage guys are great."

"I know they are good, but what did they do, there has been nothing on the news about the sighting at all and I thought there would be."

"The clever bit was the fake covering the windows on the mini-bus so it would look like a van. We had several sites reconnoitred so a quiet one could be chosen, then just change the plates and the roof stripes and bonnet covering and away we went. It looked just like the van the cops have. That stuff on the bonnet and roof is just like fablon. I think we spent thirty quid plus whatever the plates cost. How much were they?"

"The numbers cost twenty plus ten to have them made. They are available on the dark web and you just pay with a debit card, just like eBay. They even include where the vans are stored so there is no chance you will meet the clone. You also get a choice of Police, Fire or NHS; they all have plain vans, no difference in price but the police ones put them off more."

"Mark, I do think we are lucky with you. Where did you get all the clever bits from, all our family are nowhere as smart as you."

"I guess having that accident meant that I couldn't be a builder or housebreaker like the rest, so I had all the time to learn, plus the disabled charity were always keen to get me a background in IT as it meant I could work. I wonder what they would think if they knew what I do now?"

"Stop, just the thought of you on a course to learn how to buy all the illegal gear you deal with makes me nearly wet myself. Anyway well done on your side. The minibus was back to normal and back in the yard before five. Who did you get to phone the sighting in?"

"Your memory is getting bad, you got the driver to do it. I had given you a sim card to use just for that call."

"Of course silly bugger I am. It's a bit busy at the moment with 'other things'; nothing you need to know about."

"And I don't want to know, I am happy being Mark the Vape. Virtually no chance of getting done for the cannabis vape as it's in a known brand bottle and the sim cards come in boxes of 100. I wonder how they manage to clone them so easily?"

"Now that I can tell you, the phone companies get them produced by the million and the new numbers appear in batches, our suppliers just use batches that are due out in a year's time."

"OK so what do you need me to do next?"

"Get me two sim cards and two phones, but kosher ones as they are for Carl, one must be from Portugal. Can you get that?"

"No problem. The internet is wonderful for what I don't have in stock."

"OK I am off now, thanks for the tea. Let me know when I can pick up the phones and sim cards. Carl is off in about a month now so no more sightings. He had all his hair cut off the other day, apparently made all sorts of fuss. It was not as if we turned him blonde."

Naomi's Story

Had the police around today. They called and arranged a formal meeting so I could get my solicitor to be here at home, not dragged into custody this time which was a surprise.

A week ago there was a sighting of Carl. They brought pictures that they asked me to verify, and they were only a week old. The brief told me after that they had probably been following me for a week to see if I had any contact, but I had no idea.

So the old bugger is still alive. Well that makes things easier, but what on earth is he doing? I have not heard from him and I wonder if he has become involved in something really illegal, not impossible knowing Carl but to give up everything. I can't believe it.

I wonder if the sighting was planned to get me and that Jane off the hook for him disappearing. There being no evidence to tie us to the PI's murder then was Carl involved in that?

Jane's Story

This is better. It's only been a couple of weeks and things are looking up. I have two new assignments, one courtesy of my new 'partnership' with Mike and have been offered a free holiday from someone called 'Victims Charity'. It's in Portugal but I can't hold a country responsible for my troubles.

I don't believe a word of it. Carl would sell his mother for a profit but was fun to be with and we were good in bed. I wonder what has happened to his wife. I suspect she will be well looked after as he always seemed to have plenty of money and told me so. That has pushed my distrust of the police to a new high. Anything to 'close' a case it seems. I still wonder what his involvement was.

It's funny how three close brushes with the law can turn someone's head. I had not realised but several of my friends feel similarly, not as definite as me but certainly distrust.

So back to Portugal, not the Algarve, but near Porto in the north should be warm still and I am off in two weeks. The work didn't take as long as I thought. Now no picking up men at the airport. Well, actually, I wouldn't mind, it's been a while. No guys who are too good to be true. I want someone who is believable, even a good honest villain will do for a week. Actually, I have just described Carl to myself! Hey ho, that is at least a model to watch for.

Off out for a bite now with a girlfriend. Hopefully, no one will break in, be abducted or murdered while I am out. What a set of thought to have! I need that break.

So just had a call and my mate, Shirley, is going to be fifteen minutes late and I was fifteen early. Never mind, I will enjoy a glass of wine while I wait. I am a bit worried because there is a guy at the bar who has looked over a couple of times. He seems vaguely familiar as well, still I should be safe in a bar. Let's get that wine.

Well, that was a surprise, I did know him.

"You are Jane, aren't you?" (I answer yes) "What a strange co-incidence you are one of the people we want to discuss working closer with, you doing that project with Mike?" (I answer yes again).

"I am David Flowers. I work for the US part of the same company as Mike, we have an office in the same building." (Hence, the vague recognition I realise).

"It's weird bumping into you because I was just about to ask Mike for your number. One of our US subsidiaries is launching a new range footwear, padding, helmets, clothing with padding for semi-dangerous sports like skateboarding, extreme water sports, snowboarding, extreme mountain biking, These all have spine and neck protection like modern leathers for bikers."

"No one has yet done an automated series yet, high end product specification with mid-range cost because all the designs will use the same integrated support systems. It is a worldwide project, so although, it is US based, the work can be sourced from anywhere on the globe and with your record you are the ideal consultant."

I give him my number and my friend arrives, gives me a dirty look and when we are sitting down asks, "How long does it take you? I am fifteen minutes late and you have hooked up with a good looking guy already. Shall I just go home and let you two get a room?"

I explain the reasons and we have a great laugh, she still wants to know which training course to go on. 'How to pick up guys in a bar without being a tart', is her suggestion.

Two days later, David contacts me and we have a meeting, not face to face as he is in the US by then and there are two others, one in the US and another in Australia.

We agree the brief and I am appointed. I will get the component specifications and drawings by email and when I have done the task of combining what components that can be, I will be sent samples, as will the others so we can meet virtually again and discuss how best to move to manufacture.

It's probably two weeks solid work but with what I have coming, I will be kept busy for at least a month. Not sure how much time I will have on 'holiday' but at least I will be busy and not have much time for the 'men' who seem to be messing up my life at the moment.

I had better get packed as I am away in two days and have to get draft suggestion to Mike before then.

The police have given me back my passport since the sighting of Carl and I have warned them I am going away.

Detective Inspector Will Knowles and Detective Constable Susan Howe

"So bring me up to date, Susan, are we any further forward in any area?"

"Not really, Sir. We have also had to give Jane Adams back her passport, no excuse to keep it as Carl has been seen and we have no real evidence regarding the dead PI."

"So we are basically going backwards. We are having to close off the avenues of enquiry that we have and now have nothing?"

"Sorry, Sir, but that is about it. Neither we, the guys in Kent or the Midlands have got any further forward. Look, Sir, can I suggest that we all get round a table and try to work out what is going on"

"That might be an idea. What would you suggest?"

"Well, a fixed agenda around what we know as fact;"

"First that someone seemingly died in Portugal but that was faked, we know this because he died in the midlands. A woman was arrested for his faked murder and was cleared when the apparent victim died here."

"Second that the woman in question was having an affair with Carl, the wide boy who then also disappears, presumed hurt at least but probably dead. Then he reappears briefly but convincingly; both incidents involve vans, both have cloned number plates which are police numbers. Very clever and very well organised."

"Third, the private investigator who was employed by Carl's wife to trace the 'other woman' dies. We have been back through all his cases for the last five years and they are all clear and not connected. He did specialise in tracing cheating husbands and had a reputation for it."

"The only link we really have left is Naomi, Carl's wife. She has been watched on and off like a hawk and has not made one slip. She admits to getting the report from the PI and wondering what to do about it, and the next thing she knows is that the woman has seemingly been arrested."

"She did make the comment that if she was the type she would have gone after Jane but thinks that it must have been another of Carl's conquests. You know found an earring in a pocket and realised it was not the wife's somehow. Or a new perfume on his collar, or saw them together."

"He and Jane used the same gym, that was where they met so it could be another of the women at the gym, but unless we question the hundreds that go there and one lets something slip. Actually, shall I just check with the gym staff, they might have noticed something."

"Yes, on the gym staff and I will let you know in an hour or so about the meeting. Good synopsis regarding the case too."

"Thanks, Sir. I will go straight to the gym now and get the numbers of the staff who are not on duty. I think this needs speeding up, we seem to be getting mired in so much information that it is slowing us down."

The Police Meeting

"Thank you all for coming. We are it seems at the centre of an investigation into two murders; we thought three until recently as you all know. I would like to formally introduce our two sets of colleagues—Midlands police and Kent police, who both have had to deal with one very violent murder each, linked by three people—Jane Adams, Carl and Naomi Hall."

"Well done, Sir, I think that went well."

"Well, Constable, I don't think so. We are no further forward at all. We all have had to conclude that Carl has morphed from a wide boy into some sort of national criminal. I agree we had no option as the indications are clear, so we have to admit defeat and start a manhunt it seems. Are the press office getting all the information ready?"

"Yes, Sir, they are, but I don't see how we can come out badly from this? We followed all the correct procedures and it was only Carl's reappearance that has triggered this escalation."

"The press will still have a field day saying that we have been dragging our feet, calling us plods and somehow making us look bad."

"Not much we can do about that, Sir."

"No, I suppose not. It just gets to me when we can see that he must be the head of something but will probably never be found."

Carl's Story

Bloody hell, I am in trouble now. My picture is all over the TV and papers as some sort of crime lord. I will be lucky to get out of the country. I have asked to see the boss again to get some sort of sense, presumably that is why I am now bald.

Uncle Bob and His Boss

"Well, George, that went well. We are pretty much in the clear now as long as they don't get Carl."

"They won't do that, boss. If they do, he will be in a body bag and he knows it. Even if he did somehow get away then, he will be in the frame for two murders and lots of lesser crimes. That he does not know anyone's real name and we have shown him the 'evidence' that will incriminate him if he ever sings will keep him in line."

"I have booked the plastic surgeon who will alter his ears and nose so even facial recognition won't find him. I know that is a bit much but it's the price he is paying for getting the two women off."

"How did he react to that?"

"He understood. He is a bright guy and once he is set up in Portugal, he will just drift into the background."

"Do you wonder why it is so easy to fool the cops?"

"No, boss, they have to work within guidelines and we all know them, by manipulation, we can pull the wool over very easily."

"I suppose so. It's good that we have moved into the 'woke' society. It makes everyone behave the same, far fewer mavericks who would possibly get us."

"I understood that was why the organisation was set up this way. It was someone's idea and by breaking down the areas and creating sub-contractors, it meant there were never any crime lords to chase."

"Yes and I knew that guy, he did it to get himself out. He was a typical Mr Big and there were always people after him. By splitting up his empire, he created a system that works well. I believe he took his inspiration from Mrs Thatcher; she could see most things clearly and did herself get toppled. He has avoided that."

"Clever guy. I won't ask who he was it could be dangerous."

"You are correct there. The family are still directing lots of things. They set up the gang war twenty years ago which left lots of minor criminals with no direction, and by using them in their specialist areas, created the culture."

Carl's Story

I am off now to get on a light plane to take me to France and then will be driven down to Portugal. It seems that my 'injuries' are from a fall and I have the medical record and medicines, painkillers mainly, and the prescriptions, so I won't be stopped.

They have fitted me up perfectly. I now understand that this scenario had I been seen in advance. Apparently, whoever runs this lot also has a computer gaming development business, it takes all the possible scenarios and has them ready for the 'operators', so when something happens, they can stay two steps ahead by having everything planned. Very impressive.

Jane's Story

Well, here I am again at Gatwick, BA. This time not Easyjet, but it seems like it's mostly just the uniforms that are different.

No good looking guys and no women with plastic tits either which is a welcome difference.

I have the name and address of the villa that I am staying at. I have a taxi booked by the charity which will meet me at the airport so I don't have to do very much at all.

Flying is so boring. Yes, I had magazines and a book to read but there is no buzz. Well perhaps, I had better get used to that. The villa has a pool, is fully stocked with food and there are others who will be there.

We have to cater for ourselves but it's all provided. We all have en-suite rooms. There is only space for four in the villa and a representative will be there to introduce me to the others.

An hour's drive from the airport. That was quite warm and despite the air conditioning, it seemed hot. Not bad for October, much better than in the UK.

There is actually only one other here but I won't meet him yet. He is just having stiches removed after ear and nose surgery after a bad fall. I believe he may have been being chased by the police when it happened, hence the same charity have helped him.

Carl's Story

Ouch, that hurts. The nose and ears are very tender and every time I put a shirt over my head, I seem to catch something. It's getting better slowly and I won't have to worry about being recognised.

Different ears and nose, shaved head and a beard, and even I don't recognise myself. Although, they are ruthless when something goes wrong, they have a 'code' where they quietly make it up to those they have harmed and might be able to come after them, like me. Or they kill them.

So here I am in Portugal, hidden in plain sight. I am glad they were impressed with my trainer scam and decided to take it on board as a 'product line'.

I am also glad that they wanted me too, it would have been so easy for them to just dispose of me. I am looking forward to getting fitter too. The swimming pool is big enough and I have an exercise bike and rower plus weights.

This is a nice villa. I have a valid, if a bit suspect, UK passport. My Portuguese is improving and if I can pass as a native, they will turn me Portuguese they say.

All the dealings will be very tenuous. I will hardly ever see anyone and the phones are all pay as you go mobiles, except for my two official ones.

Now on consideration I am lucky. I now have the sun as well as a good lifestyle. I only need to work about twenty hours a week and I am part of an organisation. They are criminal I know but I only deal in the grey areas like I did before. If I was caught, I doubt I would go to prison even.

Naomi thinks I did a runner, understandable considering that the police think that or that I am a gang lord.

What I did find out, like I said, was that they do pay their debts. If they mess up, they cover their tracks and are not opposed to buying a bit of silence.

They have even found me a friend to stay with.

"What you up to?"

"I am going to get another cold drink. So, you want one?"

"Jane, I would love another beer. Cheers."